KISSING THE PLAYER

RULES OF THE GAME
BOOK 1

HEATHER YOUNG-NICHOLS

Kissing the Player
Rules of the Game 1
USA Today Bestselling Author
Heather Young-Nichols

All rights reserved.
Copyright © 2023 Heather Young-Nichols
Print ISBN: 979-8-9893933-3-6

heatheryoungnichols.com

ALSO BY HEATHER YOUNG-NICHOLS

Rules of the Game

Kissing the Player

Wanting the Player

Moonstruck

Moonstruck

Moontouched

The Empowered Series

The Gremlin Prince

The Goblin War

The Gorgon Sacrifice

Shadow Coven

Haunted Magic

Cursed Magic

Stolen Magic

Fated Magic

Forever 18

Forever Grayson

Forever London

Forever Lennox

Heavy Hitter

Pushing Daisies

Daisy

Van

Bonham

Daltrey

Mack

Courting Chaos

Cross

Ransom

Booker

Dixon

Finding Love

Making Her Mine

Making Him Hers

Harbor Point

Love by the Slice

Love by the Mile

Love by the Rules

Gambling on Love

Highest Bidder

Highest Stakes

Highest Reward

Holiday Bites

All I Want

All of Me

The Fallout Series

Last Good Thing

Last First Kiss

Last Chance Love

With J.A. Hardt

Bound by Magic

With Amelia J. Matthews

Dirt on the Diamond

After Office Hours: Seducing the Professor

CHAPTER 1
SILAS

*E*ither this bar was so fucking loud that my ears were going to ring later tonight, or I was getting old as fuck.

Now, normally, I didn't mind the noise or the crowd. In fact, I preferred it. Too much talking in a place like this was never a good thing—or at least, in my experience, it wasn't. Then Harlowe had to go and turn the music down a little as she called out, "For the sake of my sanity, the next person to touch that volume is going to get a front-row seat to a demonstration of my knife skills."

I snorted. Listening to a short woman threaten a bunch of professional baseball players was hilarious. Best of all, Harlowe was my sister's best friend, and

I'd known her forever. That meant I knew she'd follow through on her threat.

"What the fuck was Hanson saying to you at second today?" My best friend and teammate, Jenner Greene, took a long drink of his beer and then set the bottle down on the table louder than necessary.

"You know Hanson. Always trying to fuck up my game." Which was how it went.

Most of the time, when there was a guy on my base trash-talking, it was about normal things. Telling me I was going to choke. Saying that I owed my career to my family. Shit like that. Hanson… he made it personal as shit.

"How hard was it not to punch him in the face during the game?" Jenner had humor in his voice as he ran his hand through his messy mop of brown hair. A move that drove women crazy.

Jenner and I had grown up together. Played ball together since tee-ball. We'd been drafted to separate teams, but baseball was unpredictable and now we'd both landed on the Kalamazoo Knights. Me by design because my grandfather owned the team and dreamed of having all us boys on the same team like some kind of fucked-up legacy. So far, it was just me and my brother Brooks, who was a catcher and the oldest of the five of us. Four brothers and one sister. Unfortunate for her to have us as her brothers.

Unfortunately for all of us, my dad was such a fanatic that some of us had gotten the messed up names we had. They're fine now, but going through school… some of us had a rough time. And it was really unfortunate that my mother hadn't put her foot down until Camden. And even that was base-ball related.

Mom said Gramps was determined that this was the year she'd get the other two brothers onto our team since she ran the day-to-day now that he couldn't. Gramps was the wallet at this point. Though he'd built up a great system before having to retire.

"Almost fucking impossible," I told him honestly. "He said some shit about Camden." While he wasn't the first to do it, for some reason, when he did, it pissed me off more.

"So he has a death wish," Jenner said before tipping his bottle again. "What'd he say."

"I'm not going to fucking repeat it." That shit stained my brain, but there wasn't a chance I'd tell him.

"Well, I'm probably the only one who could tell you were holding back." Which likely wasn't true.

However, part of being a professional baseball player was shutting everything off and playing the damn game. Nothing else mattered when we were on the field.

We'd played a day game today and were only going to have one drink since the season was rough. One hundred and sixty-two games in the regular season with only around fifteen or so days off mixed in there.

"So what's the bet this year?" Jenner said now that we could hear each other.

We spent more time than we should in this bar, aptly named Cleats & Kegs, and owned by Harlowe's parents, Though I thought she might've lived here because there was never a time that we came in that she wasn't behind that bar.

"Bet?" I asked like I didn't know what he was referring to. Jenner and I made a bet at the start of every season. It was mostly stupid but gave us something fun to harass each other about. "I think we've done all of them."

Jenner scratched at the stubble on his chin. He'd shave before the game tomorrow, which was his ritual. His dark hair was darker than mine, but we'd been told more than once that we looked like we could be related. My brothers and I did all look alike. Dad used to joke that they'd had Brooks then put him in a copy machine to spit the rest of us out.

They weren't wrong. Not only did we look alike, but we all played baseball, though we weren't given much choice. It was kind of the price to be paid for being born to a mother whose family owned the Kalamazoo Knights and a father who'd set records when he'd played. Now retired, Dad thought his job was to run the rest of us and our careers.

Whether we liked it or not.

"True," Jenner agreed. "But we can recycle. What do you want to do? Most triples by the end of April?"

Triples were fucking hard. Home runs were honestly easier. Every man on a professional team had an arm like a cannon. It was hard as fuck to outrun them. But make the bet too hard, like hit for the cycle in a single game, and neither of us would win. A single, double, triple, and home run in a single game wasn't something that you could plan.

"Why don't we do RBIs? Haven't done them in a while." And they were far fucking easier than triples.

"Fine by me."

"What do I get when I win?" Because yeah, every pro player was also confident as hell. We had to be, or we'd never get up there and let some guy throw a hundred-mile-an-hour fastball at us.

Jenner snorted. "When *I* win… I get fifty thousand dollars to the charity of my choice."

I quickly agreed. "Fine. But you're not winning." That was a win-win situation. Whatever happened, a charity was getting a nice donation, which was the stake every year. I didn't know why we even talked about it anymore.

Jenner and I had placed a bet, or challenge, depending on how you looked at it, every year after the start of the season. Even back in high school. Now, the prize got bigger when we both went pro, but the spirit of the bet was the same. We'd found back then that it helped push us just that little bit harder, and it must have worked. After all, we'd made it.

And he knew I'd been on a hot streak all through spring training and during the few games we'd had. That wouldn't scare him off.

"What're you looking at?" I asked as I leaned back to see what he did.

Ah. Yeah. A group of women—five that I could see—were sitting at the corner of the bar sipping their fruity drinks and giggling when one leaned in, her lips moving quickly as she said something. The way all of their gazes came to us at the same time told me that whatever she'd said had been about us.

This wasn't unusual.

We were professional baseball players at the top of our game and in peak physical condition. It attracted all kinds of attention, including that of cleat chasers—women who wanted to be with us *because* we were baseball players—no other reason.

That shit had started in high school.

"I know you see that," Jenner said, bringing my attention back to him. "We should go talk to them. Could make for an interesting night."

"We have a game tomorrow." It was a brush-off, and I knew he was aware of our schedule. It didn't matter if we had a game tomorrow. We'd just had the first of a six-game home streak before we'd head back out onto the road.

Jenner snorted. "And that matters why?" We'd both been called up around the same time, and three years in the Major Leagues had taught us a thing or two.

To me, it didn't matter, but I wasn't in the mood tonight. Yeah, maybe that was a first for me, or it had been recently, since this season I just didn't have the same *thirst*, I guess.

I'd been the hook-up king since tenth grade. Jenner had a girlfriend since the summer before freshman year. He'd loved the hell out of that woman, so when he'd found her cheating in the fall of our senior year, he'd thrown himself into any woman who'd have him.

And he still did, swearing that he'd never open himself up to having his heart broken again.

I didn't believe him, figuring that eventually a woman would catch his heart again, but none had.

"You suddenly changing everything about yourself?" he asked, watching me for any reaction.

I sat back, as if I didn't have a care in the world and snorted. "Fuck no." That would mean wanting a relationship, and there was only one woman who could've ever been that for me. Unfortunately, I hadn't spoken to her in at least four years. Not since I'd gotten drafted in college. Even then, she'd never been anything but a friend.

And she could never be anything more. No matter how much merely thinking about touching her smooth, pale skin or feeling her lips against mine one more time made my mouth water.

I emptied my beer and then slammed it on the

table with a little more force than I'd meant to. "All right. Let's go."

Before either of us could move from our seats, two of the women we'd seen talking about us slid up to our table.

"Hi," the blonde one with the full lips said to me. "You boys look so lonely over here."

It took everything in my power not to roll my eyes. The redhead with curves for days was leaning over, talking to Jenner, no doubt giving him a full view down the front of her shirt. She slid onto his lap just as quickly as she and her friend had appeared.

The blonde cocked her head to the side for a split second before moving to do the same as her friend, only on *my* lap.

"Let me grab you a chair," I told her before reaching around to the table behind me and pulling one over. I didn't want this woman on my lap.

"You're a baseball player, right?" she asked me. I couldn't hear what Jenner and the redhead were whispering about, but given the giggles I heard from her, it wouldn't be long before the two of them left.

"I am. But I think you knew that."

It wasn't my intention to be a dick to her. All I

wanted was for her to know upfront that she wasn't going home with me. I hadn't been joking when I'd said I wasn't in the mood earlier. Or rather when I'd tried to use the excuse that we had a game tomorrow.

"Do you need another drink?" she asked. "I think we should get you another drink." She motioned to Harlowe then waited until my sister's friend appeared. "I think he needs another beer."

Harlowe raised an eyebrow my way because she knew better than anyone about the limit I had when it came to drinking. One beer on a game night and no more. Ever.

I quickly shook my head and Harlowe disappeared. "I'm good," I told the blonde whose name I hadn't asked for yet.

"So…" This was awkward as fuck, and she was feeling it too. It didn't have to be. But I was putting in exactly zero effort. "You have a game tomorrow?"

"Yup."

"You're the second baseman, right?" She was trying too hard, and it wasn't her fault.

"I am." It was time to change my perspective. Even if I didn't want to fuck this woman tonight, there was no reason to be a dick. "What's your name?"

"Brittany."

Of course it was. "I'm Silas Briggs." I reached a hand out to shake hers. She took it but blushed harder than a virgin on prom night.

"I have a confession to make," she said. "I knew that. I was kind of playing dumb so it didn't seem like I was coming over here because you're a ballplayer." She glanced at her friend, who had her tongue in Jenner's mouth. "That's her thing. Not really mine."

I raised an eyebrow because things had just gotten interesting. "No?"

She shook her head. "I'm not a hook-up person. But Andie wanted to come over here and didn't want to come alone."

Now I gave her a genuine smile. "That's perfect because it's not my thing tonight, either." But you couldn't say that Brittany wasn't Andie's ride-or-die. This could have gone very differently if I had been into it, and I began to wonder how far she would've let it go.

Morbid curiosity.

Instead, we were able to talk about normal

things. She was actually a fan of baseball and knew the game, so that was what we discussed.

Until a woman with dark hair and pale skin brushed past Jenner. He wouldn't have noticed if a bomb had gone off in the place since I'd bet my career he was about two minutes from leaving.

But this woman caught my attention.

It couldn't be her, but fuck… It was almost as if she were familiar and just the possibility of it being her had my dick hardening in my jeans.

The woman with the smooth skin and soft lips who haunted my dreams regularly.

The woman I'd kissed the night before leaving after being drafted and hadn't seen since, even though we'd been friends for years before that.

I was the dick in this situation, but fuck, I couldn't dim the hope that it was her coming back home.

Those fucking hopes were extinguished when the woman turned—It wasn't her.

This woman might've been pretty, beautiful even, to the right person.

She just wasn't Amity.

CHAPTER 2
AMITY

My stomach tightened, and I wasn't sure if it was anxiety mixed with a little excitement or if the burrito I'd eaten last night was coming back with a vengeance.

Anxiety was most likely. A burrito had never done me wrong.

I'd been back in Kalamazoo for a week but had spent most of that time setting up my apartment. Now it was time to dive into the job that had brought me back here. Which meant facing one of the reasons I'd wanted to stay away.

Before I could take another step, the shrill sound of my phone grabbed my attention.

"Hey, Dad," I answered after checking the display to see who was calling.

"Get to the stadium OK?" he asked, as if I hadn't grown up here and hadn't been to the stadium a hundred times with him since I'd been little.

"Sure did. Turns out, they didn't move it." He was just as concerned with who I would see today as I was.

My relationship with my dad was one of the best that I knew. Having that closeness meant I'd told him when Silas kissed me the night before he'd left. He knew that Silas had never called me again. We hadn't stayed in touch.

Dad was just as pissed at the guy as I was, though I'd sworn him to secrecy four years ago. He could never speak a word of how much Silas had hurt me.

I was beyond that now.

Dad's deep chuckle reminded me that I was on the phone.

"Hey, Dad," I said. "I have to go fill out paperwork and shit. Can I call you after?"

"Yeah. Make sure you do, though."

After a wholehearted promise to call him as soon as I was finished here, I ended the call.

Dad used to say I was the only thing he had left, but I insisted he would have to stop doing that once he had a girlfriend. Calling me the only thing he had left wouldn't make a woman feel very good, and the one he was seeing now was exactly what he needed. Though he swore he'd never get married again, I was working on him.

Never say never kind of thing.

After a long breath, I headed in the front entrance to the offices.

Baseball had been a part of my life since before I'd known what it was. Working in that world now… it was what I'd always wanted.

"Amity Kincaid?" the woman standing at the front desk asked before I could introduce myself. She was around my age, taller than me, which wasn't hard to achieve, with pretty, blonde hair pulled up in a bun. Her smile was kind, and I was thankful for that.

First days were hard enough without people having an attitude.

"That's me." I reached out and shook her hand as she introduced herself as Leah.

"I'm going to get you all settled today. It won't take too long." I followed as she led me down the hallway to a small office about the size of a large closet but not one of those walk-in kinds that at least had a window overlooking the field. "You lucked out," she told me. "The office is small, so most people don't want it, but you can look out onto the field."

"It's perfect," I told her, trying to keep a stupid grin from appearing. This cracker jack box was perfect for me.

She snorted. "I'm glad you think so. All right." She pulled a tablet out of the pile she'd been carrying. "This is yours. And this"—she handed me a sticky note—"is the password. You'll have to change it once you log in. But this has a great note app you can use the pen to scribble with. It sounds weird, but there will be times when you're just walking around and people need things from you. Take notes."

"I definitely will."

"Also, the first thing you need to do is fill out all the forms. It'll pop up. But we need your information to get you added to payroll."

"I'll definitely do that first."

"It *is* the most important part." She chuckled.

Yes, I might love this game, but being paid was the most important part of this whole thing. And this job was paying me more than I'd ever been paid before. I wasn't going to screw this up.

"All right." Leah sighed. "You get those filled

out, then come find me. I'll take you on a tour of the stadium."

"I've been here—"

"Doesn't matter. We go places fans don't. You have to have the tour." She glanced down at the strappy sandals I was wearing. "Also, just a tip from me to you. Bring in a pair of Converses or something you can slip on for days when you'll be running around. Your feet will thank you. Plus, they'd look cute with the skirt you're wearing right now."

"Got it."

Leah left my tiny office so that I could dive into form filling out hell.

On the phone, I'd been told that the dress code was business casual, so last night I'd laid out this dress. It looked like a skirt with a shirt tucked into the belt, but it was one piece with a light-blue top and a geometric-patterned, blue-and-white skirt. Paired with the strappy sandals, I thought it looked great. I assumed it was fine because Leah hadn't said anything about it, other than to be kind to my feet, but these sandals were quite comfortable.

After I'd finished the forms on the tablet, I headed to Leah's office. When I entered, she was on the phone and held a finger up for me to wait. Her office was as neat and organized as I imagined she was. While I waited, I made a mental note to look for a crossbody bag that would fit the tablet and my phone because carrying this around in my hands would be less than ideal.

I liked to have my hands free. What if someone handed you something and you couldn't take it because you were carrying this tablet?

"All right." She hung up the phone and grabbed something off her desk before standing and coming toward me. "Here are your credentials. You need these every day. It'll give you access to everything and also when you travel." She stopped and looked me in the eye. "They did tell you about the travel, right?"

I chuckled and said, "Yes. Travel won't be an issue."

She pushed out a breath. "Good. They forgot to tell the last assistant travel secretary, which is how the position became available again. Even though *travel* is in the title, she thought she was going to be the travel secretary's assistant. Not exactly the same thing."

"They said I'll travel sometimes, but not every road trip."

"Correct. There's a calendar on your tablet,

which you can sync to your phone if you want to, that has which trips you'll be needed on." She began walking again and I had to hurry to follow. "There's always a travel person on the road because shit goes wrong more often than you think. Sometimes it's the travel secretary, or actually, it's mostly her, but sometimes, she needs you to do it. And if an emergency arises, she'll need you to step in."

"Not a problem."

"Good. Now." She clapped her hands together. "Let's get this tour done."

Leah walked me around the entire stadium. I was very familiar with the public areas, but the staff-only areas, I wasn't. She assured me I'd get used to it quickly, and I was good with directions, so I was confident it wouldn't be a problem.

"OK." We stopped outside of a set of large, double doors. "They're in a team meeting right now that should be just about to end. The GM wanted me to introduce you to the team so they know who you are and that they can go to you with travel requests." She rolled her eyes. "There will be a bunch, and you try to accommodate, but don't break your neck trying to give everyone what they ask for. Some guys think they can have whatever they want, and sometimes they can't. Read over the travel restrictions and don't give in to them."

"Got it." I knew how superstitious baseball players were and all about their weird requests. This wouldn't be a problem.

"OK, here we go."

She pushed into a large conference room with rows of tables with mostly large guys behind them. Not all players were jacked, but they were all fit. They were all tall—to me—and they all had muscles for days, even if they were lean muscles.

It took exactly two seconds to find Silas and Jenner, who was sitting right behind him. They were in the second row to the left, and I willed myself not to give them more than a passing glance. The same as I did every player, but the sheer surprise on their faces made me stumble. Brook's had the corners of his mouth slightly upturned in a very *cat that ate the canary* semi-grin.

Jenner and Silas both had their eyebrows raised, I assumed in surprise. Both sets of eyes were wide, and both looked like they were about to say something.

I'd told no one that I was going to be working here—other than my dad—so there was no way they would've known.

While Leah introduced me, Jenner gave me a head nod, which made me smile. That smile faltered when I glanced at Silas.

He looked good.

Too damn good if I were honest with myself, which I really didn't want to be. His dark hair was shorter than it used to be and now his eyebrows were furrowed, as if he were angry with me.

There was nothing for him to be angry with *me* about, so I looked away. I hadn't been self-conscious when I'd walked in here, but the way I could feel his eyes roam over my skin had changed all that.

If things had been different, I wouldn't have regrets about losing touch with the two of them and having to follow their careers from a distance like everyone else.

Sure, I'd stayed in touch with Jenner for a while after he'd been drafted, but things had been crazy for both of us. Whereas Silas… He'd given me the best kiss of my life, then never spoken to me again.

Both had hurt, but Silas had hurt more. After all, those two had been the reason I'd gotten through the time after my brother had died and my mom had left. But I wouldn't think about that standing in front of a couple dozen professional baseball players.

The worst part of following their careers… seeing threads online of women who'd hooked up with them over the years. I wasn't stupid. I knew they'd both take advantage of being professional athletes, but following all of that—and I had followed it because I was apparently an emotional masochist—had turned me into a stupid girl who was jealous of these women for having what I never could. I was just the girl who had a crush on the boy who played on her dad's high school baseball team.

In the end, Silas had proven that I was nothing more.

Leah and I headed back up to the offices when the introductions were done.

"So spend the rest of the day acclimating yourself to the team, the stadium, your tablet. Whatever. And you can work wherever you want in the stadium. Lots of the guys sit in the stands working during warmup and batting practice. Just make sure you have your phone and tablet so you can be reached."

"Really?" I asked. "I can watch batting practice while I work?"

She nodded. "Things aren't super formal here. You can even work from home some days if you want to. We're not going to micromanage you. Plus, it's a benefit to everyone if you at least like baseball, and even if you don't, you need to know the team."

I snorted. "I like baseball."

"Excellent." She turned away then snapped her fingers and swung back around. "There's nothing official about the players being forbidden to the staffers romantically, but it's frowned upon. It can get messy."

"I don't see a problem there." Though my stomach tightened for reasons I didn't want to acknowledge. "What about friends?"

"You *want* to become friends with the players. I mean… that's fine, but they're… abrasive."

I chuckled and smiled. "I'm aware. No. It's not that I want to be friends with any of them. Friendly, sure. But my dad coached Silas and Brooks Briggs as well as Jenner Greene in high school. I grew up with those guys, though I haven't talked to either of them in years."

"Oh. That's no problem. People become friends all the time."

With that, Leah disappeared back into her office and I was on my own.

I spent a little while setting my office up the way I wanted as best I could. I made a list of the things I wanted to bring in and found the nearest restroom as well as the closest coffeemaker, though another co-worker said the Starbucks in the concourse, which would be a regular stop for me, opened early for us.

Once I'd done everything I could, I rubbed any exposed skin with sunscreen, then headed out the stadium to find a seat behind home plate—quite a few rows up so I wouldn't distract anyone—and worked there while the team tackled batting practice. Try as I might, I couldn't not watch Silas. Thankfully, my sunglasses were dark enough that he couldn't tell.

When Jenner waved, I waved back. But Silas didn't make a move to acknowledge me. When the fans started showing up, I headed back to the office. Before leaving, I stopped at Leah's and knocked on the open door.

"How was your first day?" she asked as she sat back in her chair.

"It was great. I just wanted to know if I need to do anything special to stay for the game or if I just get a ticket at the box office?"

"Oh." She came over to me and took my tablet. After opening the app she wanted, she turned it to me. "Use this app. We aren't going to make you buy a ticket. This shows you where the staff tickets are—most of the time, they're really good because they're unsold tickets. Just claim one here." She clicked through and filled in my information after choosing a seat close to the dugout. "Then just go there. Wear your badge until the ushers get to know you. You can leave your things here and get them after the game. Your badge will get you in."

"That's awesome. Thanks." Free tickets weren't a perk I'd known about before this. It was mentioned that there were games available for employees, but I didn't know it meant all of them.

After another layer of sunscreen and leaving my tablet in the office, I headed back out to the stadium. There were only a couple of hours before the sun went behind the upper deck, but until then, I was going to protect my skin.

I bought a diet pop and an order of fries, then found my seat.

It was a good game, but whatever was going on with Silas during warmup seemed to disappear. Silas hit four RBIs, but Jenner only one. They were both on a hot streak and had been getting hits and RBIs that you could set your watch to.

But there was always another game tomorrow.

After the last out in the ninth, I gathered my

trash to dump it on the way out and began to shuffle along with the rest of the fans.

"Amity," a masculine voice called out, making me cringe.

I turned to find Jenner standing on the half wall of the side of the dugout and hanging his arms over the railing.

I laughed, then headed back his way.

"Hey, girl. Why the hell didn't you call me when you got this job?" He reached out and wrapped his arms around me. I still had trash in my hands, so I couldn't return the favor.

When I stepped back, I said, "Oh, are we friends? Because that sounds like something a friend would do."

He held up his hands in defeat. "All right. I know. I suck." I tried not to notice that Silas was leaning on the front of the dugout, listening to this whole thing. "Let's rectify it. Dinner?"

"Dinner?"

"Yeah. Tonight. Now. We can get showered real quick and meet you."

I raised an eyebrow. "'We'?"

"Yeah. You, me, Silas. Like old times."

"I don't think—"

"It's a bad idea, Jenner," his deep voice said

before I could. It was a bad idea, but hearing him say it was like a knife to the gut. "You two go ahead."

"Fuck that," Jenner said over his shoulder. "I don't know what the fuck happened between you two, but you're both adults. Get over it. We'll meet you at the door in twenty."

Jenner hopped off the ledge and disappeared through the door to the clubhouse. Silas waited, his eyes scanning over me, much like they had in the meeting. It was like he wanted to say something, and yet… he didn't.

He disappeared through the clubhouse door like Jenner had.

And now I was stuck going to dinner with a man whom, for some reason, I couldn't get over.

Perfect ending to ruin a fantastic day.

CHAPTER 3
SILAS

"Why the fuck would you do that?" I spat once Jenner had caught up to me.

Going out to dinner with Amity was a fucking awful idea. The farther I stayed away from her, the better for both of us.

"What? Ask a good friend to have dinner? I know, the horror." His deadpan tone told me that he really didn't know about what had happened between the two of us. That was for the better.

"We haven't seen her in years." I stopped and put my hands on my hips. "Or *I* haven't, anyway." Then I waited with a raised eyebrow for him to tell me he hadn't seen her either. Because those two spending time together didn't sit well with me.

"I haven't seen her since we were drafted. I don't know why. I talked to her occasionally after that, but things got busy." He shrugged. "I was a shit friend." He started walking toward the clubhouse. "Amity was Jayce's sister. We should've been better friends to her."

"We were," I called out as he entered the area of the locker room where we'd shower and change. "We were good friends to her." Well, I probably hadn't been.

"Sure. For a while." He yanked his jersey off and then the undershirt. I did the same thing, then sat down to take off my cleats. "Then we got caught up in our own shit. Look." He dropped down in front of his locker. "Was there something between you two?"

I glared at him. "Why the fuck would you ask that?"

"Don't know. Seems like you're particularly sensitive about her. That usually only happens when—"

"Fuck off." I stood and whipped my belt off. Thankfully, the club handled the cleaning of our uniforms because I sure as fuck didn't want to take care of this mess.

"Hey. I had to ask." The humor in his voice

gave the anger boiling in my stomach just enough of a boost to ignite. "If you don't want to come to dinner, don't. I'm not your mother. But your actual mother would be pissed to know you treated Amity so shitily." He snorted and turned to me. "Wait until Camden finds out. You're basically dead." He slapped me on the back as he headed toward the shower. "I'm going to dinner, though, so let me know if you are before I leave your ass behind."

Fuck.

I was going. Something deep inside me yearned for the torture that would come from being around Amity.

The hot water felt good, but my mind kept drifting to Amity and the way her legs had peaked out from under the skirt she'd been wearing. She'd never been a skirt girl when she was in high school. I'd played baseball with her brother, her dad had been my coach since… well, I don't remember having another coach as a kid. Jenner, Jayce, and I had been a force on the field. In other ways too. Amity hadn't been a part of that.

When Jayce had died… Amity had been crushed, but Jenner and I had been too. The only thing that had kept us on the right path back then had been taking care of her and baseball. Somehow, her dad never missed a game, even with everything they'd been going through.

It was like he'd needed baseball as much as Jenner and I had.

Thinking of Amity while naked was a terrible idea. Our park was a little older and had communal showers. The last thing I needed was to get a fucking hard-on while in a room full of the men I played baseball with.

After cutting the water, I wrapped a towel around my waist and headed back to my locker. Jenner was already sitting in front of him with his jeans on and his phone in his hand.

"So are you going or what?" he asked without looking up.

"Yeah. I'm going." Even though I knew I shouldn't be. "Where?"

"Amity says she wants a juicy burger." He chuckled, and I wasn't about to ask why he found that funny. "How about Patty's?" I grunted my answer. Patty's had the best burgers around. We used to go there all the time when we'd been in high school and those memories were some I wished I could forget right now. "All right. She's meeting us there." He pushed to his feet and grabbed a shirt from his locker. "I offered to pick her up, but she passed." Probably worried I'd be there too. It didn't occur to me at first to ask him how he had her phone number. Now, I really wanted to know but wasn't going to ask.

Fuck, this was going to be hard.

Half an hour later, I pulled up to Patty's and cut the engine of my car.

It had been one kiss. I'd kissed Amity one time and nothing more. Why the fuck couldn't I get that out of my mind? There'd been many women since then. It just didn't make sense.

But Jenner had been right when he said she was back now. There was no way for me to avoid her. She was working for the team and *fuck*. She'd be traveling with us sometimes too.

It was almost like the universe was torturing me for having one perfect fucking kiss four years ago.

The quick knock on my window made me jump out of my skin. *Fuck.* I'd been sitting there too long. When I looked out, Jenner was standing there with his hands in his pockets and a shit-eating grin on his stupid face.

I pushed the door open hard, causing him to jump back and that could've been bad if there'd been traffic. But I had to trust that Jenner would get out of the fucking road if cars were coming.

"What the fuck are you doing out here?" he asked as I walked away from my car and hopefully left him behind. Unfortunately, he jogged to catch up to me.

"I just got here."

He snorted and I wished that I could have either punched him in the gut or turned around and walked away.

I wasn't normally a violent person. I didn't think so, anyway, but this was something else. And it all had to do with Amity.

Jenner slapped his hand against the back of my neck and squeezed roughly. "I'm so damn excited that Amity's back. I've missed that woman."

I pulled open the door to the restaurant and headed in as I asked, "Yeah? Why's that, exactly? Something happen that I don't know about?"

Jenner's loud laugh brought all the attention our way. Including hers. She already sat in a booth on the far end so that neither of us could sit next to her. Patty's was a bar and grill. Nothing fancy, but they did have some of the best burgers I'd ever had.

"Hey, Amity," Jenner greeted her as he slid into the booth.

"Hi, guys." Her voice sounded upbeat, but she

didn't smile, and it made me think about being in her position.

Here she had agreed to meet up with two guys she'd grown up with, both of whom she hadn't had contact with in a long time. At least she knew us well enough that she knew she was safe. We'd never hurt her. Not intentionally anyway.

"Hey," I said quietly. The first word I'd said to her since that night. The night that her soft skin had pressed against mine after she'd been just as excited for me about being drafted as I had been.

She'd been worried before the draft. I hadn't been. It'd been a given I was going to be drafted. All that had mattered to me that night was to where and how much. My older brother had already gone through the process and with my parents, there was no chance I wasn't going to be picked. The only thing I'd worried about had been not going before the Knights had their pick. Another team picked me first yet I still ended up here anyway. Before I'd played a single game in the majors, I'd gotten traded to the Kalamazoo Knights.

Fucking perfect.

We didn't have time for small talk before the waitress came over to take our orders. We each chose a burger with varying toppings. While Amity asked for fries, because that girl loved her fries, both Jenner and I asked for two sides of vegetables.

All part of the professional athlete gig.

"So, Amity." Jenner rested his arms on the table in front of him. "When did you get back to Kala- mazoo? Were you still in East Lansing?"

"No." She took a long drink of her water and I realized she hadn't really looked at me once yet. "I wasn't still in East Lansing. I… dropped out and moved to Grand Rapids for a while. Then Chicago."

I furrowed my brows. "You dropped out?"

Finally, her gray eyes met mine. "Yeah. You know I never really wanted to be there. I just didn't know what else I wanted to do." She sighed. "It was a waste of my dad's money and eventually, I'm going to pay him back."

Jenner and I chuckled as he said, "I bet old Stephen Kincaid has other things to say about that."

She smiled. This time, it was sincere. "He does, but he's not the boss of me."

"Right," I said while laughing.

Mr. Kincaid was tough on the field and a tough but fair parent. Though his daughter had him wrapped around his finger as a kid and I couldn't imagine that changed much.

"How is your dad?" I asked more seriously. "I haven't seen him in too long."

"He's good. Still coaching, though just high school. He doesn't do Little League anymore," she said. I'd always thought that he'd only done that because of Jayce. It made sense that a dad would want to coach his son all the way through, which Mr. Kincaid had until Jayce died when we were in high school. "He hasn't dated that I know of so if that's what you were asking, I don't know."

"*Still?*" That was genuine surprise in my voice. Kincaid had never dated someone. At least not that he'd let the kids know about. He'd lived like a monk. As if his kids and baseball were the only things he had room for in his heart.

She snickered. "No. No one that I know of since my mom." She rolled her eyes but I didn't miss the disgust in her voice when she mentioned her mom. "He still acts like I'm an emotionally injured kid whose mom just abandoned her. Says that I'm all he needs in his life."

The waitress delivered our food and we all took a bite before continuing.

"What do you think of that?" Jenner asked.

"Not a lot. I think he's probably dated and has hidden it from me." She took a quick drink to wash down the bite she'd had. "I think he needs someone in his life that takes care of him a little."

"Think he'll ever get married again?" I asked, knowing that marriage was a sore topic in the Kincaid house.

"That, I don't know. He's always insisted that he'd never get married again. That being married to my mom had killed any desire he had to do it again and since he wasn't going to have any more kids, there wasn't a point."

Yeah. That was what I'd thought she'd say.

"What was up with you during warmup?" Jenner asked me, completely changing the subject.

"No idea what you mean." I did. With the bet, he'd be watching me closely, waiting for the moment I might not be at my best so he could get ahead. I was doing the same to him.

"Yeah. You do. You were off. During batting practice, you were hitting like shit, then you go to the game and get four RBIs? Doesn't make sense, man."

I chuckled. "I just wanted you to get your hopes up, Jenner. Make you think you stand a chance of getting ahead. There was nothing wrong with me during warmup."

"You weren't doing a full swing," Amity offered, bringing our attention to her. She rolled her eyes.

"That's right." Jenner snapped his fingers. "You were there during batting practice. You saw it."

She nodded. "And he wasn't doing a full swing. That's why batting practice wasn't great."

Jenner laughed and fell back against the seat. "Having you at the games is going to be fun."

The thing neither of them knew was that I hadn't done that on purpose. I hadn't been pulling my swing at all.

It was her. Amity being there had thrown me off, and it was better that I was the only one who knew that. But now with her watching… she was going to catch everything.

She'd grown up around baseball. It'd been in their house since well before she'd been born. She knew the game. More specifically, she knew us because she'd been watching us since we were six.

I was fucked.

"Why didn't you tell us you were coming back?" I asked more quietly.

"Yeah," Jenner added. "Or tell us you were applying for this job. We could've helped."

"I got the job just fine on my own," she countered. "And why didn't I tell you I was coming back? How would I even do that? It's not like you have the same phone number you had four years ago when you were in college. We don't talk anymore. That's why I didn't tell you I was coming back. I didn't have your phone number until you sent me a text today." She leaned over the table slightly. "Which by the way, how did you get my number?"

I wanted to know that as well.

"I asked Leah."

Amity's face scrunched up in confusion. "And she gave it to you?"

"Yeah." He shrugged. "She said you told her that you knew us."

Amity shook her head then raised her hand for attention as the waitress passed us. "Could I get my check, please?"

She'd only taken like three bites of her burger.

"Is this together or separate?" the waitress asked.

Amity said, "Separate," at the same time I said, "Together."

She raised an eyebrow then narrowed her eyes. "Separate," she said again.

The waitress glanced from her to me. "I'll be right back."

Amity and I were left in a stare-down. *Fuck.* She *was* pissed if she wouldn't even let me pay for her dinner. Jenner and I had done that all the time before.

My family had more money than they'd ever be able to spend. Jenner's family was decent with his dad being a highly specialized cardiologist who had to travel sometimes for surgeries that only he could perform. His mother was a pretty prolific real estate agent. Amity had never been poor, but her dad coached high school baseball. He was paid better than most since he tended to churn out an MLB draft player every few years. My brothers and I had all been coached by him.

Fuck, we loved the guy, given that he'd stand up to my dad when Dad had given him some "tips." But it wasn't like they had the kind of money we had and none of it had meant anything to me back then.

"What the fuck happened between you two?" Jenner finally asked.

"What?" we both asked at the same time as our heads snapped toward him.

"What the fuck happened between the two of

you?" he asked again. "It's like you're both chal-lenging each other. Or trying to prove something. Fuck. I don't know. But spill. What happened?"

"Nothing," I said, then looked away casually.

"Yeah. Nothing," Amity agreed. "I think you two just got busy. We haven't talked in a while and I don't think you really know me anymore."

"We know you," I mumbled, half-hoping she wouldn't hear me and half-hoping she would.

She had. She narrowed her eyes on me.

The waitress dropped off the checks in front of each of us and before I could grab hers, Jenner did and held it out of her reach.

"Amity, let me pay for your dinner," he said in a regretful tone. "I invited you tonight. You need to let me pay."

She let out a sigh and said, "Fine." Though I had no doubt that if it had been me, she would've sat there until she was well into old age before allowing me to pay.

I'd fucked up with her.

This was my chance to make it right.

CHAPTER 4
AMITY

It was a weird feeling to be putting my own office together.

When I'd dropped out of college, my dad had been convinced that I was going to be stuck in a rut. Like him.

He loved baseball. Loved coaching baseball, but it didn't exactly pay top dollar. Even at the school that pushed out a bunch of professional players. It was still high school. He'd turned down every college job offer he'd gotten and there'd been a bunch, given his track record. He was one of the winningest coaches in the state. Beloved by players. I could've gone on.

It just wasn't the life he wanted for me. He'd wanted me to become a doctor or a lawyer—something where there'd be job security and a decent income.

I'd wanted… something different and hated that it'd taken me two years of college to figure that out. What a waste. And I'd meant what I'd said last night. I was paying my dad back one day.

This job was part of that plan.

"Hey!" a sweet, familiar voice said from the hallway. I turned to find Camden Briggs leaning against the doorjamb.

Camden was on the shorter side, like me, with dark hair—currently in a ponytail hanging past her shoulders—and beautiful hazel eyes. Her lips curved into a small grin. She was also Silas's younger sister.

"Hi. I wondered when I'd see you around here."

She snorted. "Please. I hardly ever come to the ballpark. It's random chance that I'm even here."

"Really?" I cocked my head to the side. "You could live here. Your family owns it. It's beautiful."

She rolled her eyes and sighed as she came farther into my office. "Yeah. Yeah. You know I've always wanted to stay as far away from baseball as humanly possible."

That was true. She'd been forced to come watch her brothers and with four playing baseball, that was a lot of games. She'd basically lived at the ball diamond growing up and had hated every second of it. Though I didn't think it was the game she hated, but the boys who played it.

It was how I'd come to know her. We were three years apart, which would make her… twenty-one now. I'd gone to the games because Silas, Jenner, and my brother had been playing and I'd loved it. We'd been the only girls around our age we could stand. Though we hadn't really been friends outside of that, I'd always thought we could be.

A lot of secrets had been spilled during the games. She'd even come with her parents to the college games, though by then, I'd thought she could've refused, but her dad was pretty demanding. She'd said it had been easier to give in on the smaller things so she could battle the bigger ones.

"It's really good to see you," I told her right before she pulled me into a surprising, tight hug. The girl was stronger than she looked.

"It's good to see you." She dropped into a chair by my desk, so I did the same. "When I heard that you'd been hired here, I couldn't believe it. I thought you'd never come back to town."

"Yeah. I thought that for a while, too, but here I am."

"Was it the job that brought you here?" she asked quietly. Everyone knew about my brother when it'd happened, and that had been the moment that I'd wanted to leave. I hadn't thought I'd be back either. "Or…" She trailed off.

I rolled my eyes. "It was just time to come home. I wasn't seeing my dad enough and felt guilty for leaving him alone. But it was also the job. When I saw the posting…" I shook my head. "Anyway. I'm here. What have you been doing?"

I assumed she was still in school. All of the Briggses had gone to college, though Camden was the only one expected to finish.

"School. You know."

I did. The pressure on her was just as heavy as that on her brothers. It was just pushing her in a different direction. No one expected her to play in the majors. They expect her to major in business and join the family on the team on the backend.

"So…" I traced circles on my desk as I watched her roll her eyes again.

"I'm not dating anyone if that's what you're trying to ask without asking."

I snorted. We knew each other well enough.

"Why not?"

Camden was a beautiful woman. Athletic, knew

sports—especially baseball, obviously—and she was funny and smart. It didn't make sense that she wouldn't have guys falling all over themselves to be with her.

"I could ask you the same thing," she answered instead.

I pulled back, like I was offended. "How do you know I'm not seeing someone?"

Camden dropped her head to the side and raised an eyebrow. OK. She had me there.

"I don't know why," I told her. "No one has asked in a long time."

"I find that hard to believe."

Now I had to laugh. She could see right through me, apparently. "OK. No one worth saying *yes* to has asked in long time."

"Now that, I can believe." Then she let out a long sigh. "I don't know." She shrugged. "It seems like guys are more interested in my family than me and I'm not going to be a portal for anyone to have access to the great Conrad Briggs."

Yeah. Her dad was a Hall of Fame player and I would've bet my entire year's salary that many, many guys, both players and non-players, would give their left nuts to have access to that man.

"Men suck," I told her instead.

"That they do." We fell silent for a few moments, probably so each of us could quietly catalog our personal experiences that had taught us that men sucked. "OK." She slapped the arms on the chair she sat in. "We should go out. A girls' night. Friday night. The team's in a home stretch, so I know you don't have to prep any last-minute travel plans."

"I don't know."

Camden pushed out of her seat. "Amity, you're going to want some friends here, right? I doubt you have any."

"Ouch." But she wasn't wrong.

She rolled her eyes again. "When you lived here before you spent all of your time with your brother and mine. And Jenner. You need some girlfriends. I'll introduce you to my best friend, Harlowe. Her family owns Cleats & Kegs."

After taking far too long to think about it, I finally said, "OK. One drink."

"You can have zero drinks, as far as I'm concerned. It's about bonding."

We both chuckled.

"By the way," she continued, "my mom was so excited when she saw that you'd applied for this job."

I furrowed my brows. Why would the owner even know that I'd submitted my resume? I hadn't thought they were that involved in that kind of day-to-day.

"She only knew you did because she and the head of HR are friends. Becky asked Mom if she'd ever heard of you because your school and my brother's matched up. The years overlapped, which made her wonder if you knew each other."

"I didn't think your mom liked me."

Camden snorted. "She did. She doesn't show it well because she works so much. Even when she's not working, her brain is. Mom only had time to love us. That's the limit. No one else could have her affection. She has a great resting bitch face."

"I need your phone number," I told her. If we were going out, it only made sense to have it.

"I'll text you. What's your number?" I rattled it off as she typed then my phone did the chime that told me I had a text.

It's me bitch. That was the text she sent. I chuckled as she waved goodbye and left my office.

Camden was a different kind of woman. Always had been. She and I could go the entire winter without speaking, but once baseball season had started, we'd be close for the entire season. Then we wouldn't talk until the next season.

Somehow, that weird bonding ritual back then meant we were friends now.

She wasn't wrong. I did need some friends here.

It wasn't twenty minutes later that Jenner breezed through my open door while I typed away on my computer. I was still trying to get the lay of the land.

I was going to have to rethink keeping the door open, but I liked hearing what was going on throughout the office. Being the new girl who hid away in her office away from everyone else didn't seem like the best way to make nice with the coworkers.

Being seen as the office bitch had backfired once. I wasn't going to let it happen again.

"Hey." He dropped into the same chair that Camden had vacated. Jenner's brown hair was a mess and… slightly damp around the edges. His green eyes twinkled with flecks of brown. Probably his eyes would've been considered hazel, but there was more green than brown, so I said *green*.

"Hey." When he didn't say anything else, I sighed. "Aren't you supposed to be… I don't know… working? Workout? Batting Practice?"

"Both are already done. I'm about to get ready for warmup."

Without meaning to, I glanced at the clock. Right. I hadn't realized so much of the day was gone already and since it was an early start day—four o'clock—he would be starting warmup soon.

I turned to him and folded my hands on my desk. "To what do I owe the pleasure of a visit from the starting shortstop of the Kalamazoo Knights?"

He chuckled. "I have a favor to ask."

"Of course you do." I waved my fingers to get him to hurry up.

"I need you to fuck with Silas."

"What?" I tried not to laugh uncomfortably.

"I need you to fuck with Silas."

"No. Anything else?"

Those green eyes narrowed on me, making me have to fight the urge to squirm. In the old days, I would've been on board with whatever Jenner had planned. Now, I didn't want any part of anything that would bring me closer to Silas.

"Come on, Amity." He groaned. "I need your help. He's kicking my ass."

"Play better," I told him.

"Is Amity Kincaid too chicken to help me out?"

I rolled my eyes exaggeratedly. This was the

problem with being around people you knew too long. "I'm not *scared* to help you. I don't *want* to help you. And if you think you can goad me into it, you're sadly mistaken. I'm not a kid trying to keep up with the older boys anymore."

"Listen." He moved so that his arms rested on his knees. "I think something happened between the two of you. I don't know what, but something." He paused, like he thought I was going to fill him in, and that was never going to happen. It'd been one kiss. One. Nothing else, and being upset about it four years later was actually kind of childish. But it wasn't the kiss I was upset about. "Fine." He sighed. "Don't tell me, but whatever it was, you being back has thrown him a little. You'd be able to mess with his game."

I sat back and pressed my fingers together beneath my chin like I was some evil mastermind. "Are you saying you want me to screw with one of the best players on a team that I now work for? Losing teams have cuts. Not really with office staff, but I'm not taking that chance."

Jenner's eyes widened. "No. I don't want you to fuck him up so badly that we lose. Just so that he slows down or I'm not going to be able to catch up. It's RBIs this year. I can catch up right now, but that fucker is on fire. I need him to still get hits without driving every fucking run in."

I shook my head as I pulled my chair closer to my desk. "You're crazy, Jenner. You want him driving runs in. That's what wins games and right now, you guys have a fantastic record. Don't fuck that up."

"Can't you just flirt a little? Try to be sexy? That's all it would take. I don't know what happened between the two of you, but he's not over it, either."

Either. As if *I* weren't over it. *Fuck.* Why did he have to know me so well?

"No. I can't." Because that would be awkward, though I had to fight a laugh at Jenner telling me to *try* to be sexy. To him, there wasn't much I could ever do to actually be sexy, even if I did try. Jenner and I had never felt even the smallest tingling for one another.

My eyes had always been on Silas.

He groaned. "Fine." Then he stood like he was going to leave but turned back. "You know we're both glad you're back, right?"

"Sure." I didn't believe Silas was.

"We are. He's just gotten grumpy in his old age," he said. Now I had to snort. They were both twenty-four. Not exactly old enough to start collecting social security. "He has. I don't know why, but I roll with it because he's my best friend." He snapped his fingers. "Why did we lose contact? I'm pretty sure I sent some texts that never got answered."

Now I sighed. This was always going to come up and without Silas around was probably the better time.

"Exactly that. You were his best friend. Not mine. Sides were going to be chosen and I knew you'd choose his, so I made the decision for you. It was easier."

Jenner ran his tongue over his bottom lip, a move that had sent so many women directly to his bed. "I was your friend too. One of your best friends, I thought. You shouldn't make decisions for other people."

Then he left.

It was the first time that I considered that I could've been the asshole in this scenario.

I'd had to cut Silas off because he'd played with my feelings. He might've been the only one to know that I'd had this monstrous crush on him, but he'd known. He'd used that crush to kiss me that night. Told me he'd had to do it at least once because he'd never forgive himself if he didn't. Then he'd never spoken to me again.

Fuck Silas Briggs and fuck their bet.

Messing with him—flirting and being sexy—was a good way to start a fire I wasn't going to be able to put out, which would leave me the one being hurt.

I wasn't about to get burned again.

CHAPTER 5
SILAS

"I don't think I've ever seen you look this miserable with so many ripe women hanging around," Brooks, the oldest of the Briggs clan, said while slapping me on the back with his meaty hand.

All the brothers looked similar. At least we looked related with the dark hair and eye color that obviously belonged to the same family. Mine were dark, almost onyx, while Brooks's were what my mother called "russet."

Brooks had been drafted directly onto Mom's team and had only played here his entire career. It'd been seven years. Well… several of those had been on the farm teams, but he'd been catching in the majors since he was twenty. Seven years squatted behind home plate aged a man. Or at least aged his knees.

Not to mention high school. It all added up.

That amount of stress on the body had him working out like a maniac to keep healthy. Though he'd never have a serious injury unless he caught a bat to the head.

"Fuck off," I muttered.

He wasn't wrong. Usually, when there were willing women around, I took full advantage. Though it had started to change this season, there was one auburn-haired reason that I couldn't even look at another woman right now.

Cleats & Kegs was busy tonight. *Fuck.* It was usually busy, but we had an unusual day game, which meant the entire team had time on their hands tonight. After another day game tomorrow, we were traveling on Monday. The entire team wasn't here. Some of us had wives and families to spend time with, but there was enough of us that I was keeping my eye on Amity.

The idea of one of those fuckers even talking to her burned my stomach.

Brooks dropped into the chair next to me. Jenner was across from us.

"He's been distracted," Jenner told him, like I wasn't sitting right there.

"I have a lot on my mind," I told them, though I wouldn't say what or I'd never hear the end of it. "May I remind you… I didn't even want to be here." Meaning the team, not the bar.

Brooks chuckled. "You've got to get over it, man. The team needs you." He rested his hand on my shoulder again.

"Fuck off." I shrugged so his hand would fall off. "You know I give everything every single day. That's not what I meant. I didn't want to be playing on Mom's team. Where Dad has too much influence."

Nodding knowingly, Brooks took a drink before he spoke again. "None of us do, but it's fucking inevitable. You know that. We all know that. Mom and Dad can't be what's distracting you from hooking up tonight."

That… I wasn't going to answer.

"What do you think's going to happen when your brothers are all brought to the team?" Jenner asked as his gaze slid over the ass of the woman who'd just passed our table.

"Fuck." Brooks chuckled. "They're going to be so pissed. Urban's going to fight that pretty hard. But we all know it's going to happen. Mom's going to shell out big bucks to make Dad's dream come true. Even Urban won't be able to say *no* to it."

"The way Cobb is pitching right now, it's going to be a *lot* of fucking money."

It was like we'd been on a baseball pipeline when we were kids. Dad had started us before we could even join a team. He'd been determined to produce a bunch of baseball-playing boys. His full dream had almost been realized, then Camden turned out to be a girl.

He wanted the legacy.

The baseball royalty family—and we were required to be good. He'd lucked out because we all did actually love playing baseball and we were all good. Which was part of the reason we loved it so much.

We just all could do without the constant pressure he liked to exert over us. *Fuck.* He'd even wanted to handpick our agents when we'd been drafted, yet not one of us had gone with his choice.

Dad had been so set on his baseball progenies that he'd named most of us after players. Mom had gotten to name me after Grandpa, who owned the team, and I was the only one she'd named. Dad had chosen Cobb after Ty Cobb, Urban after Urban Shocker, and Brooks after Brooks Robinson.

That was when the laugh I'd grown to love as a teenager floated above all the other noise.

Amity's laugh was distinct in that it was all-encompassing. If anyone heard it, they usually laughed along with her. It was infectious.

Her auburn hair brushed over her shoulders in waves and the way her smile took over her whole face hit me in the gut.

Fuck. She was beautiful, and I was a damn creep for watching her the way I was.

"Hello…" Jenner waved his hand in front of my face. "Did you even hear what we said?"

"No." I tipped the bottle of beer against my lips.

"That's too bad. It was hilarious."

Jenner shook his head, but Brooks had this cocky half-grin on his face. Fuck him.

"What were you staring at?" Jenner made a point of looking around until he found exactly what had gotten my attention.

"The women are here," he said, stating the obvious. "I don't know how you two do it. If my little sister was here surrounded by all these fuckers, I'd haul her ass out."

So would I, except for one thing. "Camden hates baseball players," I told him. "She'd rather admit herself to a nunnery than date a player, so we're good."

"Plus, this is her best friend's place," Brooks added. "Or, rather, her parents' place. Harlowe works here. You know what the fuck I meant."

We both did, and we both already knew that Harlowe was here more than anyone. The woman worked hard, but when she dropped into the booth next to my sister and wrapped her arm around her shoulders, I was reminded that no matter how hard she worked, she'd always made time for my sister.

"Isn't that what they all say?" Jenner asked, causing Brooks and me to furrow our brows. "That they hate ballplayers. Until they sit on one of our dicks."

I groaned. "No, fucker. They don't *all* say that, and if you even hint at my sister sitting on anyone's dick, we're going to have to have a chat. With my fists."

"Ditto," Brooks added.

We all knew Camden dated, but not a single one of us brothers wanted to fucking hear about her sex life.

Jenner chuckled, then pulled a tall brunette into his lap. I would've intervened, but she'd been making a move on him all night and giggled as she landed.

Not wanting to be here in the first place took a dive as I watched Amity throw back shots. That woman didn't drink much, so the fact that she was had my antennae raised. What was she trying to run from?

"Can't take your eyes off her, huh?" Brooks asked more quietly.

Shit. I needed to do something about that. So instead, I looked somewhere else. Anywhere else. Which only made my brother chuckle.

"You should just throw her over your shoulder and take her back to your cave like the caveman you are," he advised.

"I don't know what the fuck you're talking about." Unfortunately, his plan sounded like exactly what I wanted to do.

"Sure, you don't. You've wanted Amity for as long as I can remember. Probably as long as *you* can remember."

That wasn't something I'd admit to. Not to anyone, and now I wondered how many other people had noticed. No one recently, that was for sure.

"Listen." My brother moved in and crossed his

arms in front of him as a woman walked by and trailed her fingertips across my shoulders to get my attention. She wasn't getting it. "Is this still about her brother?" My jaw tightened. "You need to let it go, man. It wasn't your fault."

Through clenched teeth, I said, "Change the fucking subject."

As if he'd heard me, Jenner came up for air with the brunette and said, "Who's leading the race right now, Silas?"

Fucker. He was and he knew it, but by one RBI.

"Oh, that's right." He snapped his fingers. "I am."

"It's one run, asshole. I'll pass you tomorrow."

"Sure, you will."

"I'll be right back." I sighed as I pushed to my feet.

I didn't even need to use the bathroom, but it got me the fuck away from my brother and my best friend. If Jenner paid attention to anything other than baseball and pussy, he would've overheard Brooks, and I never would have heard the end of it.

If Jenner knew that I could get hard just *thinking* about Amity, he'd use that to his advantage.

As I washed my hands, the door to the restroom opened and a brunette with blue strands tucked throughout her hair slipped in. She was taller than Amity. Curvier too, but the fact that I was comparing her to Amity in my head was fucked up and showed that I wasn't interested. Even if the thought of fucking Amity out of my system with someone else was kind of appealing.

"Hey," she said, the corners of her mouth turning up. She had on a pair of pretty short jean shorts with this black, lacey top that just looked like a bra with this flowy jacket kind of thing over it. It wasn't thick like a jacket, though. Actually, it was so thin, it was almost see-through and it was longer than the shorts.

"I think you've got the wrong restroom," I told her as I finished washing my hands.

"I definitely have the right one." She stepped closer and rested her hands on my chest. "Watching you play is…" Her gaze slid down my body then back up. "Such a turn on. I thought we could have some fun."

There'd been a time I probably would've taken that offer, but tonight wasn't the night, and I was not the one.

"If you're looking to fuck a ballplayer, there are plenty out there." I pointed back out to the bar.

She scrunched up her face in disgust. "I don't want to fuck a ballplayer. I want to fuck *you*."

"Then you're going to have to learn to live with disappointment." I moved to get past her, but she moved too. The irony of the fact that if I were her in this situation and I was the one getting in *her* way of leaving, that would've made me a fucking predator. "Listen, I'm not fucking you tonight or ever and I'm certainly not fucking you in the restroom at a bar."

"I've been told I have a really talented tongue." She ran that tongue over her top lip as if to demonstrate the point.

I shook my head. "I'm sure you do, and you should probably use it on someone who'd appreciate it. Tonight's not the night, and I'm not the one. Now I'm going to walk out of this restroom, and you're going to let me."

This time, she didn't try to stop me, but she slid in front of me so that she'd exit first. I didn't care what people thought we'd done in that restroom and it was about time for me to get the fuck out of the bar anyway.

CHAPTER 6
AMITY

*L*ook at me pretending that I'm not being tortured by sitting in a bar with Camden Briggs and her best friend, Harlowe Chandler—who also worked at said bar.

Camden and I had been sitting in this booth for about twenty minutes before Harlowe had joined us. She had a break, she'd said. I tossed back a second shot hoping that the burning liquid would lessen the amount of torture I was going through.

Oh, right. I didn't mention the fact that Silas was halfway across the bar with his brother and Jenner. That wouldn't have anything to do with what I was feeling, now would it?

It took everything in my power to keep myself from glancing over at him and I'd already lost the battle three times. Though it seemed like *he* was watching *me*.

"I know I shouldn't say this," Harlowe began, "mostly because the whole baseball thing is likely why we're still in business…" I raised an eyebrow at her. It was a silent question as to what she meant. "Oh, the guys come here because it's not as crowded as other places. It's almost like we're *their* bar and of course the women follow." She rolled her eyes.

"You don't like baseball players?" I asked, taking a small sip of my margarita. Damn, that was good and I wasn't even a big drinker.

Camden snorted. "She *loves* baseball players."

"Excuse me." Harlowe held up a finger. "I don't *love* baseball players. Are they sexy as hell? Yes. But it's not like you can insert any player here and I'm running off to the bathroom with him."

"That's true."

Camden and I snickered. "You were saying," she said, twirling her finger in the air as she took a drink of her own margarita.

"Oh, right. I know they're the reason we do as well as we do, but sometimes… I wish the cleat chasers would stay home."

"Amen to that." Camden reached her hand up, which Harlowe immediately high-fived.

"They can't all be bad," I told her.

"They're not. They actually tip pretty well and everything, but fuck, I hate cleaning the bathroom knowing what's happened in there."

My eyes widened. I knew the stories of the random hookups and also knew they happened. My brother had been the high school version of the guy she was talking about, but these were grown-ass men. They couldn't really have been hooking up in the *bathroom*.

As if reading my thoughts, Camden said, "Oh, it happens." Then she pointed down this little hallway where the restrooms were. A petite blonde was righting her clothes then ran a finger around her lip liner to make sure it was in place. She was followed by the Knights center fielder, who was tucking himself back into his jeans.

Gross.

"I stand corrected," I muttered into my glass. The girls giggled.

Camden patted my arm like she was soothing me. "Yeah, you have to get used to being around them again."

She was right. I did have to get used to it, but

seeing Silas do those things was going to be so much harder.

"Anyway, tomorrow's a travel day," Camden said, changing the subject. "Are you on this trip?"

"Yes." I cleared my throat. Finally. Something I wanted to talk about. "Patty, the travel secretary, can't make this one. Actually, she said if I work out the way she thinks I will, she'll have me split the travel more evenly. Or even take over if I want to. She doesn't love being away from home so much."

"Yeah. It's a lot and I go sometimes with Mom and Dad." She rolled her eyes. "They're both convinced that I could take over for Mom one day."

My eyes widened in excitement. "You want to run a baseball team?"

"No." She shook her head. "Or I don't know. I don't think so, but it's a long way off. The way they see it, we all need to be involved in baseball somehow."

"You're an adult," Harlowe countered. "You could come work here."

"I know. But they're playing Cobb's team on this trip and sometimes it's the only way I can see my brothers. Their schedules are insane."

That much was true. We talked a little more about the trip before Harlowe had to go back to work. Once again, I found myself glancing over at Silas. It was like I couldn't forget he was there.

Lucky me.

When I looked at him again, it was just in time to see a woman trail her fingers across his shoulders. The only positive here was that he didn't seem to notice—at least, he certainly didn't acknowledge it.

My stomach started to hurt like that time I'd gotten the flu. I'd thrown up more than I'd known I'd had inside me. This time, I wasn't sick in that way. It was the combination of alcohol and Silas.

"You know this is why I won't date one of them," Camden said, snapping my attention back to her.

"What?" I used the straw to mix up the frozen pebbles of ice in the margarita and to avoid looking at her.

"The guy coming out of the bathroom. My brothers and Jenner with the women all over them. That's why I won't date a player."

I snorted. "I'm sure that makes your brothers very happy."

Now she chuckled. "It does. Sometimes, I think about bringing one to a family thing just to fuck with them."

I began laughing too. Silas would lose his shit,

as would the rest of the Briggs boys. "If you do that, I want to be there." Then I realized what I'd said and shook my head. "At least take video."

Camden watched me as if she were trying to figure something out, then she wet her bottom lip and leaned forward. "What's going on between you and my brother?"

I furrowed my brows. "Nothing. I've barely spoken to Brooks since I got the job."

She shook her head. "You know that's not who I'm talking about. Silas. What's going on between the two of you?"

"Nothing." I said it so immediately that at first, I didn't notice how sad my voice sounded at the fact that there was nothing going on between us.

"Something did, though, right?" she prodded. I was about to deny that when she held her hand up. "I've been around, remember. I know that you were around him and Jenner a lot because of your brother." My heart clenched at the mention of my brother. "Then everything happened and it was like you never spoke to him again. Or, rather, I never saw you all together again."

It had to be alcohol, but there was suddenly a nagging in the pit of my stomach that I needed to tell someone what had happened. I hadn't before this—other than my dad—but for some reason, I thought I could trust Camden.

Still, I said, "I can trust you, right? This goes no further?"

"Absolutely," she said. Then I glanced at Harlowe as she walked by. "Not even to her."

After swallowing hard, I started. "I did still see the guys sometimes. But after my brother died… I don't think anyone knew how to handle it. My mother left because she didn't know how to handle it and said looking at me was too painful."

"That's awful," she whispered as she laid a hand over mine.

"So there were a lot of things happening at once. My brother, my parents' divorce, my mother never wanting to see me again. My dad was trying to take care of me while also grieving himself. That's why he went back to the team so quickly. The season was underway and it gave him something to focus on."

"I don't remember seeing you at the games that year."

I shook my head. "I couldn't go. It was too much."

"I'm really sorry, Amity."

I gave her a grateful smile then continued. If I

was going to tell her, it had to be now. "I didn't see the guys much after, but I also didn't *never* see them again. Jenner checked on me the most. Said he and Silas had always promised to look out for me and Jayce had promised to look out for you, so he came around. Your brother didn't because Jenner said he felt too guilty, but he would never tell me why."

"Probably because he felt he didn't do enough to try to save him." She sighed. That sounded like the Silas that I knew.

"Anyway, Silas came to see me alone the night he was drafted." I took a deep, cleansing breath. "He kissed me that night. It was… There was so much behind it that even after four years, I can't put words to it. In that moment, it meant everything to me." I shrugged. "In the end, it meant nothing and I didn't talk to him again until I got this job."

Camden winced as anger flooded her features. "So he did a drive-by kiss? What a jerk."

"I'd had a crush on him since forever and he probably knew it. Jenner was like another brother to me, but Silas…" I shook my head because I couldn't allow myself to fall into those thoughts right now. "Anyway, I thought it meant he liked me, but clearly, it didn't. I just have no idea why it happened or why he seemed so angry about it when *he* kissed *me*. It was four years ago, so it's done and over with, but he's weird as hell with me. Almost like he's still angry at me for something, but I didn't do anything."

At that moment, my stomach decided to remind me that it wasn't all that happy. Could it have been the chicken wings with super-hot sauce I'd eaten? It absolutely could be. When I went to excuse myself, a cramp like no other took over and I thought I was about to let loose on the table. Instead of saying anything, I just got up and headed for the restroom, hoping my stomach would hold out.

Right before I was going to push through the door, the men's room door opened up and a brunette walked out with Silas right behind her. She adjusted the bra top she had on and gave me a cocky grin, like she wanted me to know exactly what they'd been up to in there.

My stomach turned again and I hurried into the ladies' room.

"Amity?" Camden called after me.

I barely made it to the toilet, dropping to my knees so hard that they were going to bruise, and emptied the entire contents of my stomach in one motion.

Alcohol, hot wings, seeing Silas after he'd

fucked a random woman in the restroom when he knew I was there… it all could've been a factor.

And who knew if she *was* random. I didn't actually know if he had a girlfriend because we weren't in a place where I could ask. If I even wanted to know.

Another wave ran through me as the door to the restroom opened and someone came in. I hadn't had a chance to shut the stall door, so they definitely found an unpleasant sight. Whoever it was pulled my hair back so that it was out of my face and that was a moment of women helping women right there.

Except it wasn't.

When I glanced up to thank whoever it was, Silas was the one squatted down next to me with my hair in his hand. I groaned and turned back to the toilet. He rubbed my back until the dry heaves subsided and I was able to sit up with my feet out in front of me and my back against the wall.

Without a word, Silas went over to the dispenser to get a paper towel, ran it under some water, then brought it back to me.

Once again, he squatted down to my level putting himself so much closer to me than he should have been.

"Thanks," I said weakly.

"Really shouldn't be throwing those shots back," he told me, which caused me to scowl. He was the reason I'd done it in the first place.

"I normally don't."

"And that's why you're in here."

I shook my head trying to rid myself of this feeling like I was going to cry. It wasn't him. It was that I'd just thrown up. Or that was what I told myself, but being close to him threw my emotions into overdrive and I didn't like it at all. "Isn't your woman waiting for you?"

He scowled back. "I don't have a woman."

"Didn't look that way to me when you were coming out of the bathroom."

"You saw what you wanted to see."

"I—" No. This wasn't worth the argument and whether I was going to argue or not didn't matter because he cut me off.

"Remember you said we were only friends?"

My eyes widened. "You hear what you want to hear. I didn't say that." I pushed to my feet but still had to lean against the wall for support when the room tilted slightly. Silas followed. "I reminded you that *you* said we were only friends."

"Same thing."

"Is not." Well, that made me sound about eight years old. I blew out a breath to calm myself. "You used it as an excuse and then were pissed at me. Seems like you still are."

His jaw tightened, but he didn't say anything because what could he say? I was right. There'd been something off about Silas since my brother had died that went beyond the normal grief for his friend. He wouldn't tell me what, though, and I couldn't allow him to play with my feelings again.

We were past that or at least we should have been.

"Are you all right?" he asked instead of further engaging, though this was the closest I'd been to him since I'd come back.

"I'm fine. Just a bad combination of hot sauce and alcohol."

Our eyes locked and it had me wishing that I could read him as well as I used to. I knew the boy he'd been. This man standing in front of me… he was mostly a stranger, though, I thought that boy was still in there somewhere.

Neither the boy nor the man wanted me and that was something I was going to have to get past. We had to work with each other sometimes and we'd have to be grown-ups.

"Are you going home after this?" he asked, though I couldn't imagine why he wanted to know, so I nodded slowly. "Are you driving?"

I shook my head softly. "Camden picked me up."

He wet his lips and gave me a curt nod. "I'll make sure she's OK to drive."

Then he left the bathroom without a glance back.

It took me a couple of minutes to splash water on my face and rinse my mouth enough that I felt slightly human enough to go back out there. This time, I didn't try to pretend that I wasn't looking for Silas, but he wasn't anywhere I could see.

Camden stood next to the booth with her purse across her chest waiting for me.

"Are you all right?" she asked when I got to her.

"I'm OK. Just a bad night."

"Are you sure?" she pressed. I nodded. "OK, well, I'm under strict instructions to take you right home." She put her arm around my shoulders and began to lead me from the bar. Once we were in her car, she said, "My brother was adamant that I get you right home. What happened between you two? I was headed to the bathroom when he went in after you so I hung back."

I laid my head against the cool glass and told her, "Nothing good. Nothing helpful."

But tomorrow, I'd have to act like this hadn't happened and we hadn't had the conversation we'd had.

Tomorrow, I'd have to pretend like Silas Briggs hadn't just suggested that we'd have been together now if he hadn't thought I'd said it would ruin our friendship then.

Tomorrow, I'd act like I wasn't still in love with Silas Briggs.

CHAPTER 7
SILAS

I never should've gone into that fucking bathroom last night.

Taking care of Amity was second nature. That wasn't something I'd ever regret. Seeing her on the floor huddled over that toilet had simultaneously pissed me off and made me want to take care of her.

My regret was over the fact that it'd been too intimate. Too much like something a boyfriend would have done. Or fuck, a friend. We weren't anything. We were people who'd once known each other and nothing more. We could never be more because she'd kick my ass to the curb if she ever found out I was the reason her brother had been killed.

I wouldn't survive that.

After talking to Camden, I dropped back into the seat at a much more crowded table with my brother and Jenner. I didn't hear another word said to me and left soon after.

The next day was a travel day, but we weren't flying out until the late morning. I wanted to get a workout in first, so I showed up at the field early to use the equipment. Needed to work off some of this pent-up Amity energy.

But of course she was one of the first people I saw in the hall on the way to the gym. She was talking to Patty, our travel secretary, and it seemed like a relaxed conversation. It made me wonder if Amity was travelling with us this trip. Patty usually went, but sometimes, her assistant did.

The last thing I needed was Amity in a hotel hundreds of miles from home, where no one would see us. Even if it was just a three-game series in New York.

Fuck.

I needed to pound the track of the treadmill immediately.

After a quick, thirty-minute run at a faster pace than I normally set, I let the treadmill slow and come to a stop. It felt good, but my brother was leaning against the front of the treadmill, his hair slightly damp, like he'd been working out too.

Funny. I hadn't seen him in here when I'd arrived.

"What are you punishing yourself over?" Brooks asked before running a towel over his face so he didn't see my reaction.

"I'm not punishing myself." I stepped off the equipment, hoping that Brooks would let it go. Talking about Amity… *thinking* about Amity was the reason I was here in the first place. When she hadn't lived here, hadn't fucking worked for the team I played for, it had been so much easier to push her out of my mind. Now she was every-fucking-where and I couldn't avoid it.

Brook snorted. "Sure, you're not. It wouldn't have anything to do with the woman who followed you to the restroom last night, would it?"

"Nope."

I headed over to the weights thinking that if I was working out, he'd leave me alone. Unfortunately, Brooks's only talent bigger than baseball was annoying the fuck out of me when we were working out. Usually, it was all about how he could lift more longer, but today… it wasn't going to be that.

"So what happened in the men's room at Cleats & Kegs?"

"Not a fucking thing." At least it was honest. Nothing had happened in the men's room.

"I saw the woman follow you in. She came out before you." He snorted as he alternated arm curls the way I was. "I have to admit… it seemed pretty fast, but hey. They can't all be five stars, am I right?"

I stopped and put the weights back on the shelf with more force than I should have. "This wasn't anything. She followed me in. I told her to fuck off. That's it."

"Problems?" He raised an eyebrow.

"Jesus-fucking-Christ." I sighed then pinched the bridge of my nose before looking at him again. "I didn't fuck that woman. I told her to fuck off. I didn't want to fuck her. Not that I couldn't have."

He stopped the weights. "You took a while to come back. I saw you stop to talk to Camden, then she and Amity left. So what happened?"

This was my older brother. He and I were the oldest two and had been close since birth. He knew everything about me except how I felt about Amity. Then or now. I didn't want that to change.

"When the woman finally got the message, she

left the men's room and I did too. It looked like we were coming out together." I glanced around to make sure no one was close by. Thankfully, Brooks and I were the only ones still in the gym. "But then Amity hurried into the women's room and I heard her throwing up. I just went in to make sure she was all right."

Brooks set the weights on the shelf with a loud clank. "You've got it bad, man."

I furrowed my brows. "Because I made sure she's OK?"

He shook his head. "Nah. You've always had it bad for Amity. She's great, though, so you might want to hop on that before you miss your chance again."

My jaw tensed to keep me from entertaining the idea that I could be with her and to control my anger toward my brother. "I'm not *missing* anything."

Fucking liar. Not being with Amity meant I was missing *everything*, but this was one aspect of my life where I couldn't give in to what I wanted.

"Besides," I continued, "even if I did want her, you know that could never happen and you know why."

Now it was his turn to furrow his brows in

confusion. "Is this the Jayce bullshit?" he asked and it took everything in my power not to put my fist through his teeth. I wasn't normally a violent person, but there were two subjects that could get me there. "You've got to let it go, man. That shit wasn't your fault."

"You weren't there," I said more quietly. "You don't know what happened. If Amity knew that the whole thing was my fault, she'd hate me forever for killing her brother." I took a deep breath and started to walk away then thought better of it and turned back to him. "I just really need you to let it go."

Then I went to take a shower. If my brother knew what was good for him, he'd drop the subject entirely.

Our appearance code wasn't strict, but we all had to look put-together. I typically traveled in dress pants and a button-up shirt. Most of the time, I rolled the sleeves up. Something my mother called "business casual."

To avoid everyone and everything, I shoved earbuds in and listened to a podcast so no one would bother me. On the bus, I settled back with a sigh. This road trip, though quick, was the break I was going to need. No Amity. No thinking about her. Just baseball, which is exactly where my focus should've been. I was two **RBI**s behind Jenner and while I didn't care about donating to his charity, I did care about him beating me.

What can I say? Baseball players are competitive.

All those plans went out the window when Amity climbed onto the bus that was taking us to the airport. That meant she was going on this trip and I was going to find out why.

I grabbed my phone.

Why is Amity on the bus? My sister should know. They were hanging out together a bunch now.

My phone vibrated. *Uh… because she's a travel secretary.*

Yeah. Obvious answer. Peggy went on the trips most of the time. She was an older woman who reminded me of the house mothers sororities had. She was nice and organized but could be quite firm.

Yeah, no shit, I sent her. *But usually, Peggy comes.*

Amity looked down at her phone then typed something and I had to wonder if Camden was texting her right then too. She could've been searching for ways to dispose of my body for all I knew but my gut told me it had to do with my sister.

In almost no time, my phone buzzed again. *It's a

quick trip. Amity said Peggy wanted her to have a dry run on a trip that wasn't too long. This way, Amity can get a feel for everything.

Well, damn. There went my plans of not thinking about the woman. My phone vibrated again. *Btw, I'll be there too so I can see Cobb.*

Well, fuck my life. The two of them were going to be the death of me.

Somehow, I was able to successfully avoid my sister and Amity the entire first day that we were in New York. I saw Cobb for a while then Brooks, Jenner, and I went out, got food, went to some of the places we liked best around the city then turned in early since we'd have to be at the park in the morning. Cobb wasn't there because he had some extra team shit to do.

We did our normal workout, then batting practice.

That was where my streak ended.

As we practiced, Amity and Camden were sitting behind home plate, talking and laughing and barely watching batting practice.

I'm not normally full of myself, but people come to batting practice to watch. Instead, Amity had her feet on the back of a chair, her auburn hair pulled up in a bun, a tablet on her lap, and sunglasses on her nose, so I wouldn't really know if she was watching or not. But they were giggling and their fucking giggles were annoying the shit out of me.

Jenner was at the plate while Brooks stood near where the on-deck circle would be when Benny Garcia and Trever Lowenstein joined us. They were on New York's team and why they were out here while we were taking batting practice, I didn't know. Normally, that didn't happen. Now Trevor was the second-best pitcher on the team right after our brother Cobb. He wasn't pitching tonight, but Cobb was.

"Do you know who that is?" Trevor asked, pushing his chin toward Amity and Camden. "She's fine as hell."

My stomach tightened as Brooks said, "Which one? I don't think either answer is going to do you any favors, though."

He wasn't wrong. I'd hold back violence if he was talking about Amity, but I sure as fuck didn't want him leering at my sister, either. At least I knew she wouldn't go for a ballplayer.

"You better not be talking about my sister," Cobb said suddenly so neither of us had to. "What's up, brother?" He glanced at Brooks. "Or *brothers*?"

The three of us chuckled as he hugged me then Brooks.

Cobb was the youngest of our group. Only twenty-three and had been pitching in New York for two years. Not to mention he was on track to be the best pitcher in baseball. Maybe not this year, but overall. It was still too early to tell this year and I'd do my best tonight to remind him that I was still his older brother.

"So," Cobb said back to Trevor. The way he was standing, he looked so much like Dad. Tall, dark hair and eyes, but all of us had that. It was his mannerisms that were most like our father's and likely he'd end up in the Hall of Fame just like him. "Who were you talking about? Not my sister, I hope."

"Your sister?" Benny asked with a smirk.

"Yeah. One is our sister. The other is someone we've known forever, so she may as well be family. So which is it?" Cobb stepped toward his teammate. Trevor was only about an inch shorter, so I wasn't sure Cobb was intimidating, but there were three of us and there was security in the fact that not a one of us were going to throw a punch. Not on a game day and for Cobb, he should avoid it altogether.

"The one on the right."

Brooks made a loud sound like a buzzer going off. "Wrong answer. That's our sister."

"Damn," Trevor muttered and he shook his head before walking away, leaving the three of us chuckling.

"I wonder why he didn't change his sights to Amity," Cobb said, but he laughed while I scowled.

"I think that might be a touchy subject." Brooks wasn't even trying to hide the humor in his voice as he nodded his head toward me.

"Oh, really?"

"Can you two shut the fuck up?" I snapped. "Batting practice. You aren't even supposed to be out here. Aren't you pitching tonight?"

Cobb smiled a toothy grin. "I am. I feel like it's going to be a no-no."

I shook my head. There was no way he was getting a no-hitter tonight. "Good thing I'm here to crush your dreams," I told him.

"Cobb!" Camden's shriek brought all of our attention to her. Even those on the field. She hurried down the steps as Amity watched and flung herself into her brother's arms. She was still in the seating area, but it worked. She hadn't seen him yet because she'd come in this morning with our parents.

Those two were only two years apart and had grown up close. We were all close, to be honest, but they'd been at home when the rest of us weren't.

At least she got to see him before the game.

Once the game started, it was all business.

And fuck if he wasn't right earlier. We were in the fifth inning and so far, the bastard had thrown a no-hitter. The fact that he'd struck Brooks out was something he was going to hear about the next time we were together. I'd popped out and been thrown out at first.

Fuck. I'd wanted a hit this time.

I was batting third this inning, so I waited near the steps of the dugout when Brooks approached me.

He said, "You want it bad, don't you?"

"Fuck yes. The last thing I want is for my little brother to throw a no-no while we're playing against him. What kind of message does that send?"

Brooks chuckled as I glanced to the right, where Camden was without Amity. Those two had become close and it was weird seeing one without the other in the stands.

"You know if you remove your head from your ass, you might be playing better," he told me.

Fighting the urge to flip him off, I shook my head. "Is that what the whole team has to do? Because if you haven't noticed, no one, including you, has gotten a hit."

"That's true. I also only had one at bat."

Well, fuck. He had me there. Brooks had caught a bat to the helmet when he'd been catching in the third inning and had to be pulled to get checked out. He was fine, but once you're pulled, you're pulled.

"Is this supposed to be a pep talk?" I asked, watching the guy before me take a swing. I needed to get on deck.

"You're distracted. Your crush is hopeless and apparently all you can focus on," he said. My crush? Fuck off. "Fuck her and get it over with."

Instead of tossing out any comebacks, I stepped out to practice my swing.

But what Brooks had suggested wasn't exactly the worst idea.

Fuck Amity and get her out of my system.

But I couldn't do that. I couldn't fuck Amity without one of us getting attached.

For now, I had to put it all out of my mind. Camden called out all of her encouragement, yet last time she'd done that with me, she'd also cheered when Cobb had gotten a strike on me. But I had a feeling this was going to be the one.

At the plate, Cobb tipped his hat and tried to keep the smile off his face. He was in game mode, yet we were still brothers.

The first pitch wasn't good enough. I took the strike. He knew what I wanted and was going to give me something close that wasn't actually it to see if I'd reach. It was the second pitch that spoke to me.

I swung, made contact, the sound of the bat hitting the ball was a sound that I loved the most. And that ball took off. It climbed and I knew it was going out. You can tell. The way it leaves the bat, a player can tell if he needs to haul ass to base or if this was going to be a home run.

It went into the seats.

When I looked at Cobb, he was only smiling a little. After all, the cameras were on him right now. I dropped my bat and shrugged then took off to round the bases.

No way was I letting him get a no-hitter on my watch. Against another team? Absolutely. I'd be proud as hell.

After stepping on the plate, I went back to the

dugout. Just in time to see Amity leading our utility player out of the dugout.

Fuck, that pissed me off, even though I knew nothing was going to happen. Madden might not have been playing that day, but he wasn't going to go off and fuck the travel secretary during the game. I didn't think Amity would do that, either. I couldn't know for sure, but she sure as hell didn't scream hookups.

I'd thought nothing would fuck with me more than seeing her before the game.

I'd been wrong.

We ended up winning, but I didn't see Amity again until later. During the game, Madden had come back, but Amity hadn't.

When I found her in the hallway at the hotel— she was on the same floor I was—I couldn't help myself.

"Do you enjoy tormenting me?" I asked, but she had her back to me and luckily, the hallway was empty.

She turned with wide eyes. "What?"

"Tormenting? You like that? It could fuck with my game."

Her mouth opened like she was going to say

something, then her lips pursed and she folded her arms under her breasts.

"I'm sure I don't know what you're talking about."

"Madden. During the game. Going off with him?" God, I was an asshole. Even to my ears, that sounded like I was accusing her of something. Which I had no right to do.

"Madden?" she asked, as if she didn't understand. "I was doing my job. His passport is expired and we need to renew it for the Toronto series. That's what I was doing today. Reviewing everyone's documents."

"Seems like you enjoyed havin' him alone."

Now she scowled and I knew I'd pissed her off. Good. If we were angry with each other, things would be easier. "As much as you enjoyed having that woman alone in the men's room the other night."

Now I was pissed. "I told you that you see what you want to see. You saw me near her and what? Assumed I fucked her in the men's room?" The way her jaw tightened, I knew I'd pissed her off good.

"Fuck you, Silas. I enjoy my job, yes. Does it put me alone with players sometimes, also yes. But, unlike you, I don't randomly fuck someone because they're in close proximity. My standards are a little higher."

Then she turned and stomped away.

Yet I couldn't keep myself from watching the sway of her hips and the movement of her ass.

No. This hadn't worked in helping me put Amity Kincaid out of my mind. The opposite was true.

It had turned me on so much that I was standing in a hotel hallway with the hardest erection of my life.

CHAPTER 8
AMITY

*W*ell, that was not how I'd seen my night ending.

Being basically yelled at by Silas Briggs for doing my damn job had definitely rocked my confidence.

Where the hell had that come from anyway? I had to talk to players about travel. It was literally my job. Why did he care, anyway? We weren't together and weren't ever going to be together. It shouldn't have mattered to him if I was hooking up with random people.

Someone knocked on my door and I wasn't in the mood for it. I yanked the door open to find Camden standing on the other side with raised eyebrows.

"Hey," she said tentatively.

"Sorry." I turned back into my room.

Camden came inside and shut the door quietly behind her. My anger was boiling inside of me and I needed to let it free, but she wasn't the Briggs who deserved to be the target. Camden had been nothing but nice to me since I'd gotten back to town and we'd become friends.

"What's going on?" she asked as she came to a stop an arm's length away from me.

"Nothing," I snapped, then I released the tension in my muscles. "Sorry. I didn't mean to snap at you."

She sighed. "Let me guess… my brother?" My gaze collided with hers, but I didn't answer. She sat on the edge of my bed and said, "Now, normally, I'd have to ask which brother, but this time… it's Silas. We both know it's Silas. What'd the dickhead do?"

"Nothing." I dropped down on the other end of the bed. "It doesn't matter."

"It does. I'll kick him in the nuts later for you, but how hard I'll kick him depends on what he did."

I snorted because there was a good chance that Camden meant what she'd said. "You don't have to kick him in the nuts on my account, but if you do accidentally do it, record it. We can have a viewing party."

We may have laughed, but then she nudged me with her shoulder.

"How about we go grab a drink really quick?"

Now that, I could get behind.

The two of us made our way down to the bar in the hotel without running into any of the players. We grabbed a booth and ordered a glass of wine. It wasn't until after our first sip that she dove in.

"No, really. What'd he do?"

After a long sigh, I filled her in on our interaction out in the hallway and she was appropriately irritated.

"I can't believe that jerk." She reached over and put her hand on mine. "My brothers can be such assholes."

"Yeah."

"But I don't think they're bad," she said. I didn't think they were, either. "I mostly think they don't know how to process their own emotions. I don't know. I'm not a psych major." She grew quiet for a moment before hitting me with a whopper. "And Silas, specifically when it comes to you… I think he doesn't know what to do with his feelings for you."

I held a hand up to stop her from going any further. "Nope. We're not doing that."

"What?"

"The whole *he hits you because he likes you* bullshit that people tell little girls. Silas isn't a dick to me because he likes me. He's a dick to me because… well, I don't know why, but it's not that."

Slowly, Camden swirled her wine in the glass like she was thinking it over. "I'm not doing that. Or I'm not trying to, anyway. But I knew back when you came to the games when he was playing for your dad that he had a thing for you."

I rolled my eyes and decided to be totally truthful with her. "I definitely had a thing for him, but he never gave me a second look. Whether he found me repulsive or because I was one of his best friends' sister, I don't know."

"Or you were oblivious to how he was looking at you because at the time, I didn't know much about guys, but I knew then he was looking at you like he wished he could pull you close and never let go."

My cheeks burned, but I hoped it was just something I was feeling and not something I was showing.

After quickly wetting my lips, I told her,

"Remember, I told you what happened at Cletes & Kegs. That he kissed me the night he was drafted." Another drink of wine went down all too easily because I was suddenly parched.

She cocked her head to the side and examined me. My face, anyway, for signs of what, I didn't know. "He kissed you. Doesn't that alone tell you he had feelings?" I shrugged. "I know he carries a lot of guilt about your brother, though I don't know why. Sometimes I wish I could crawl around inside his head to figure this man out. But maybe you should make a move. See what happens."

"Uh. No. First of all, my self-esteem couldn't handle that rejection. Second, I have this job now. We couldn't be anything if we wanted to. We work for the organization."

She chuckled. "I don't know. I think rules can be bent for love. And I think you're forgetting that Silas's mother, who adores you, *runs* the organization."

"Love? I think you're delusional."

Camden's phone dinged, so she pulled it out of her pocket and groaned. "I'm sorry. I have to go." We slid out of the booth at the same time, then she looped her arm through mine. "I came to your room to see if you wanted to go to dinner. My brothers and I are going out. What are the chances I could convince you to go with us?"

"Zero," I answered immediately. There was no way I could sit at a table with Silas right now, so while she headed to the front of the hotel, where her brothers were likely waiting, I started for the elevator.

Once up on my floor, the doors opened and a woman slid in before I could get out. Her hair was a mess, her clothes were disheveled, and she was running her finger around her lips the way a woman did when she was making sure her lipstick wasn't outside of her lip liner. It made me pause and reminded me of seeing Silas come out of the men's room with that woman.

"What can I say?" the woman said to me. "I like ballplayers."

Before the doors closed, I slipped out without responding to her.

Back in my room, I showered and turned everything off before sliding into my bed. But I couldn't fall asleep because of Silas on the brain.

He'd said that I saw what I wanted to see. What did that mean? That was always his response. *You see what you want to see.*

It took far too long before the meaning sunk in.

I'd seen him with a woman after they'd had random sex in the men's room. If that was what I'd wanted to see—though I rejected that notion because I *never* wanted to see him with someone else. I'd done that in high school and hadn't liked it.

But if that wasn't the truth, what was?

That he hadn't had sex with that woman. That something else had passed between them. Maybe she'd gone in there looking for an easy hookup and he'd rejected her.

But why had she been fixing her clothes when she'd come out?

Maybe because she'd wanted everyone to think they *had* hooked up.

I pictured that moment in my head and realized that Silas sure as hell hadn't looked satisfied. He hadn't had that relaxed look of a man who'd just gotten off. Then he'd followed me into the women's room to take care of me. Again, not really something I would've expected from a guy who had just been with another woman.

Maybe if I were his sister, but I definitely wasn't.

Which meant Silas was an asshole for what he'd said to me in the hallway, but he wasn't the asshole I'd thought he was before that.

The woman had played the scene. Nothing more.

Still, I didn't want to face him unless I had to for work so that he couldn't hurt my feelings again.

I grabbed my phone and pulled up the text to Camden.

I'm not going to the game tomorrow. Or the next day, but I'd tell her that tomorrow. I wouldn't be at any more games that I didn't have to attend for the foreseeable future. The stadium had offices for the visiting team. I'd work there but I wouldn't be at the game.

And now I was even more pissed at the man for ruining the game I'd been raised on and had loved since before I could walk.

It wasn't late yet and since I couldn't fall asleep, I decided to call my dad.

"I was hoping I'd hear from you, sweetheart," Dad said.

"You know the phone works both ways." Dad called me often, but he also never wanted to feel like he was taking me away from whatever I had going on. "What's new with you?"

"Well, I actually had hoped to snag some time before you left because there's something I want to tell you," he said. My stomach tightened so hard, I thought I might throw up. He'd used the same wording when he'd told me that Mom had left in the middle of the night and wouldn't be back. Now, nothing like that was going on, but those words brought up bad memories.

"Um, you were busy with the team before I left."

"I know."

"What's going on, Dad?" Then I waited for something awful.

"I've met a woman and have been dating her for a few weeks."

Silence hung between us because I was still expecting the other shoe to drop. When he didn't drop it, I said, "And?"

"I want you to know. I think she's going to be around for a while."

In all the years since my mother had left, my father had not introduced me a single woman he'd dated. If he'd dated anyone. I didn't really know.

"I think that's great."

"Really?

"Yeah, Dad. I mean, I'm not going to call her 'Mommy' or anything, but you should have someone in your life. I'm happy for you."

"Are you sure? It's been a while since there was someone in my life other than you." Which confirmed he hadn't been dating—not seriously—and just not telling me.

"It's been seven years, Dad. You deserve to have this in your life. If you're happy, I'm happy. What's her name?"

"Diane." Then he went on to talk about her like he was in high school with his first crush.

It kind of was like that. He'd been married to Mom for a while and when she'd left, it had hit him out of nowhere and crushed him. I wished it hadn't taken this long for him to meet someone, but at least he had that now.

We talked for a while before I yawned and he insisted on ending the call so that I could sleep.

My father having a girlfriend reminded me that I didn't have anyone in my life. While I didn't need to have a man in my life, I wanted one. I liked the cuddling at night, waking up wrapped in his arms. Or I missed the *idea* that I could have that, given the men I'd dated hadn't lasted long enough to really get to that point.

I'd dated. Had sex. Months had gone by, but we hadn't spent the night.

The problem was that none of them had been Silas Briggs and my stupid heart had still been set on him.

What was worse than seeing Amity every-fucking-where?

Not seeing her at all.

After our interaction in the hallway, I went to dinner with two of my brothers and my sister. Camden was sort of giving me the cold shoulder, but that wasn't unusual for her, so I didn't ask. One of us was typically pissing her off in some way.

Then the next day, Camden was alone at the game and after. There wasn't a chance in hell I was going to ask, but fuck, did I want to know.

Somehow, I needed to get over this. What I'd said to Amity had crossed a line and any feelings I had for her needed to be pushed down and forgotten about. Jayce would've kicked my ass for talking to his sister that way and while I needed to stay away from her so she didn't find out that I was the reason her brother was dead, I also didn't need to be an asshole. He'd want me to protect her feelings as much as her well-being.

Our game was over—we'd lost—and it was maybe ten that night. We'd have a day game tomorrow then head back to Michigan, but tonight, I felt like taking a swim and the pool at the hotel was still open for a while. After changing into my swim trunks, I headed down.

The pool was inside but looked like it was in a greenhouse. The three walls and ceiling were glass or something like it, which meant it felt a little like swimming outside in the night air. Not that you could see stars or anything, given that we were in the city.

When I pushed through the door, I quickly came to a stop.

Amity was on the edge of the pool with her feet in the water up to her knees. She wasn't in a swim-suit, but rather a short dress that was pulled up her thighs so it wouldn't get wet. Her auburn hair was hanging over her shoulders creating a kind of curtain around her and her shoulders were slumped

—a dead giveaway that she was either sad or reflective.

I could read her so well.

She didn't pay any attention to me coming in, which meant she either hadn't heard me or didn't care. My heart beat a little faster.

What had her down? Had someone done something? It was probably me, but fuck, I wanted to know and make her feel better.

Amity only looked at me when I sat down beside her and put my own feet in the water. Then her gray eyes slid up to find mine. When she realized it was me, she put her palms on the ground, like she was going to get up.

"Don't go," I said quietly. "Please."

She contemplated that for a few moments before she moved her hands back to her lap. "I figured I'd get out of your way," she said.

"I don't want you out of my way." And that was among the most honest things I'd said to her since she'd come back. She'd been haunting my dreams every night, but I'd been doing everything I could to push her away. It might've finally worked and now I wanted to kick my own ass. "What's going on? You don't look happy."

"I'm happy," she said, giving me the biggest smile she could muster. "I've got a great job, even if I have to work with assholes." That got me a pointed look. I'd have bet my entire contract on the fact that every single other person had been perfectly nice to her.

"Yeah. I'm sorry about yesterday in the hallway." Though I hoped like hell she wouldn't make me explain more than that.

Amity silently nodded and her silence was hard for me to take. It made me uneasy. Her angry or yelling at me would've been better. "Did you really think I grabbed Madden during the game to have sex with him?"

"No." That had been my jealousy and a way to put distance between us.

"You didn't have sex with that woman at the bar that night?" Then she groaned and looked out over the water. "I shouldn't even care. Forget I asked."

"Hey." I slid my hand under her chin so that I could turn her face back toward me. "No. I didn't. Have I done that before, sure. But I didn't that night and never with her."

"That's why you said I see what I want to see, right? Because you knew I'd make that assumption."

"*Everyone* would've made that assumption. I

could've just told you that I didn't." But I fucking loved that she cared whether I had or not.

Amity blew out a quick breath then a smile played at the corners of her lips as she focused on the water once again. "My dad has a girlfriend."

I chuckled. I'd known that man most of my life, given that I'd played with Jayce since tee-ball. He hadn't even dated after Amity's mom had left. At least not that I knew of. "What?"

She nodded. "He told me last night. Was worried I'd be upset."

"Are you?"

"Hell no." Her answer was immediate. "My mother isn't worth pining over, but he had all those years he thought they were forever. I'm glad he finally did it."

"What do you know about her?"

She kicked her legs in the water one at a time, creating a small wave. "Her name is Diane. She's a teacher, but not at his school and he met her at a baseball game a couple of weeks ago. Apparently, they've been out like six times in the last two weeks."

"Sounds like love." I'd meant it with humor and hoped she'd take it that way.

"Maybe. I'm sure it'll take him a little while to

allow himself to feel it, though. He was burned pretty badly," she said. That much was true. "Anyway, I'll head to my room so that you can swim in peace. That's why you came down here, right?"

Given that I had my swim trunks on along with a T-shirt, it was obvious, but I also didn't want her to leave yet couldn't ask her to stay. Even the smallest taste of Amity would fuck me up. I'd have to be all in if that happened, but I couldn't be. She'd hate me if she knew the truth.

She pulled her legs out of the water and stood. Without thinking, I grabbed her hand when she went to move away.

"We're good, then, yeah?" I asked because I couldn't have her walking around hating me, even though that should've been easier.

"Are you going to be a dick to me again?"

"No."

She shrugged. "Then we're good."

She walked away and I yanked off my shirt to dive into the water, but the feel of her skin on mine burned its mark into my hand and it lingered long after she'd gone.

The next day, I had my bag packed up and was ready to head to the field when I saw my brother come out of Amity's room. I dropped my bag in the hallway right outside of her door and folded my arms as I gave Brooks a stare-down.

He gave me a cocky grin in return.

"What're you doing?" I asked. We'd leave from the field to go to the bus then to the airport to head back home, so we wouldn't be coming back here.

"What do you mean?"

"In Amity's room. What're you doing, Brooks?" Not for a second did I think he'd gone in there to hook up. That would have been an insane thought and I'd recently learned that my jealousy was unfounded as well as irrational.

That didn't mean he wasn't up to something else.

"Oh, that." He folded his big arms over his chest in echo of the position I was in, so I released my arms. "Looking for Camden. She said she was swinging by Amity's room and I thought I'd catch her. Wanted to talk to her about her flight home."

I wasn't sure I believed him. All of that could've been handled with a phone call or fuck, a text.

"When are you going to sack up?" he asked and I knew exactly what he was talking about.

The problem with having brothers was that even though I hadn't spoken my feelings for Amity a single time out loud in my life, they knew me too well and could read through my actions.

"I don't know what you're talking about." Though he wouldn't believe that for a single second and when he snorted, I knew I was right.

"You know." He took a step closer. "If you're really not interested in that woman, there are plenty of people who would be. Maybe people who stayed away because they know exactly what you feel for her. Maybe those people won't stay away forever and will shoot their shot."

A fire burned in my gut with a new rage that I didn't want to contain. "Are you saying you're interested in Amity?'

He held his hands up in defense. "I didn't say me. What I said is *people*."

Now I moved closer to him. Since we were matched in height, we were basically nose to nose. "Find someone else. I swear to God, Brooks... Find someone else."

He grinned, as if he weren't bothered at all by this situation and given our past history, he probably wasn't.

Brooks was the oldest. He'd kick our asses when we were kids and needed it. He was used to managing us. Too bad for him because I wasn't a little kid anymore and while we hadn't been phys-ical as adults, I'd go there if I had to. Didn't want to but would.

The door to Amity's room flung open. "What are you two doing out here? Why are you yelling?"

Brooks's smile grew wider as he stepped back. "Nothing's going on out here, sweetheart. Just brothers being brothers."

Sweetheart, my ass. Brooks walked away, but his fucking laugh echoed down the hallway.

"Silas?" Amity asked with her eyebrows raised.

Fuck. I couldn't do this.

I slid into her room, not thinking about my bag on the floor, and quickly shut the door behind me. Louder than necessary, but that part, I didn't care about.

"What did Brooks want?"

Now her brows furrowed. "He was looking for Camden. Thought she was here, but she left already. What's going on between the two of you?"

"Nothing. Brother shit." I paced back and forth as she watched until I came to a stop facing her with my hands on my hips. "You're so fucking distracting."

"What?" She held her hands up. "I don't know what Jenner did or said, but I'm not part of that."

Now it was my turn to be confused. "What the fuck are you talking about?"

"Jenner," she said. Well, that helped not at all, so I waited for more explanation. "Jenner came to me asked me to distract you. Mess with your head so that you'd lose the bet. I thought it was because I was back in town and we all haven't seen each other in a long time, but I told him *no*. I didn't want to be part of that. I didn't want to try to be distracting."

God damned Jenner putting her in that position.

I snorted. "You don't have to *try*, sweetheart. You're fucking distracting."

She threw her hands in the air then dropped them in frustration. "I don't see how. I'm merely existing. We're not even friends anymore. How could I be distracting you unless you just really hate the sight of me?"

Oh, fuck. If she knew just how much I *loved* the fucking sight of her.

After two steps putting me closer, I said quietly, "You're distracting because I've wanted you since high school. You've distracted me since day one. I can't get you out of my mind, no matter what I do."

She snorted. "You're crazy. Are you trying to hurt me? Is this fun for you?"

I snapped my head back as if she'd slapped me. "What?"

"Tell me that you wanted me since high school? That's not remotely true. You never gave me a second glance. I was your best friend's little sister. Coach's daughter. The girl that was always around. I dressed more like you and Jayce and Jenner than I did the girls in school back then. You're saying this to hurt me, and I don't understand why."

I took another small step, which put me so close we were almost touching. "Not fucking true. I looked at you twice. Hell, I looked at you three times every chance I got. I pictured you when I jacked off back then. Imagined that it was your hand doing the work and not mine." I took her hand in mine and threaded our fingers together while holding them up to make my point. I would've given my left nut back then if it meant she would've touched me. "I was a fucking kid. Dumb. The things I thought I was supposed to want… the unspoken rules I thought I was supposed to follow so I didn't fuck up my spot on the team or my friendship with your brother… The only thing I wanted was you. But the only thing I didn't want to do was hurt you."

Her mouth parted as her breath quickened. "You wouldn't have hurt me."

"I would have. I will now, which is why I shouldn't want you. If you knew..." I shook my head. This was enough truth for one day. My guilt over Jayce, my feeling of responsibility in his death would have to wait.

"If I knew what, Silas?" she asked.

"Another time." Because everything would've been ruined if I told her right now and I couldn't take that. I was strong in a lot of ways, but when it came to Amity, I was a weak man.

"We need to stay away from each other," she whispered. "It's the only way this will stop."

I pulled her to me, dropping her hand and wrapping one of mine around her back. The other pushed into her hair as I leaned in and ran my nose up her neck and cheek. Her breath caught, and her fingers curled into the shirt covering my shoulder.

"I can't stay away from you," I whispered, as if someone else would hear me. Somewhere along the way in this room, I'd decided to say fuck it to everything I knew was right.

"What do we do, then?" Her wide, gray eyes looked up at me with both heat and fear. If she thought I was actually going to push her away right now, she was crazy. I had Amity Kincaid in my arms and even if only for a little while, I wasn't letting her go any sooner than I had to.

Instead, I tilted her head back and pressed my lips to hers.

Amity tasted like cherry. It had to be her lip gloss, but I didn't fucking care. I devoured it. I savored it as I took the kiss deeper. She readily opened up for me as she pushed to her toes to reach me better. She was quite a bit shorter than I was and I didn't want her to strain, so I moved us over to the bed with the intention of kissing her a little while longer.

Except once we were on the bed—I was half on top of her and half on the bed—she made this small noise that shot right to my cock. I slid a hand up her outer thigh and under the skirt on her sundress. God, I loved sundress season.

Her head dropped back against the bed as she sucked in air. I kissed down her neck to her chest then nipped the swells of her breast. I wanted her naked but didn't have the time I'd want to spend on her. Especially if this was only going to happen once, I wanted the night. Or the weekend. Or something other than this.

That didn't mean I wasn't going to leave my mark.

I kissed down her body over her dress while her fingers threaded into my hair and curled. It was unbelievable luck that she wasn't stopping me and when my name fell from her mouth, nothing else would stop me, either.

Quickly, I slid her panties down and tossed them into the unknown then spread her legs wide. There she was spread out before me like a buffet and I was one lucky man. I memorized her pretty pussy for when I was lonely later then licked her from bottom to top.

Nothing had ever tasted better.

Due to the lack of time I had, I went right for her clit, flattening my tongue and going to town. She squirmed and groaned, made sounds that had me wanting to cum in my jeans like a teenager. First, I pushed one finger into her then a second because I needed her to cum before I went to the field. This was my priority and when she did, it felt like I'd hit a grand slam and won the fucking game.

Her fingers tightened in my hair. Her back arched and muscles tensed. Her moans turned into my name like a prayer from her lips.

Once the waves had subsided, I pulled my

fingers out and dropped kisses on my way back up until I could take her lips again.

But then it was time to leave.

"I have to go," I told her quietly before pushing off her. This ride to the field was going to be painful. I didn't think I'd ever been so hard in my life.

"What?" She pulled her legs together and sat up. "You're leaving?"

"Got to get to the field." I adjusted myself before slowly moving toward the door.

"What?" She still sounded confused. "I mean, I know you have a game, but… what?"

"I shouldn't have let it go that far," I lied. "We work for the same place. Could get complicated."

She furrowed her brows. "You think I'm going to file sexual harassment?"

I snorted. "No. But there are rules." I ran my tongue over my bottom lip as I pulled the door open. "I'll see you later."

Before the door closed, I heard her mutter *what* again.

I did have to go, but for the first time in my life, the baseball field was the last place I wanted to be.

CHAPTER 10
AMITY

Silas just left me there in that hotel room panty-less after making me cum harder than I ever had.

It's not surprising considering that I could still feel the kiss he gave me four years ago.

Why the hell did I let him affect me this way when I knew he was going to leave me hanging there? Just like he had four years ago.

I'd assumed it would be explosive between us, but knowing was different. I'd never had a man bring me to orgasm so quickly. Those moments alone together were something I wouldn't soon forget.

For now, I needed to get my bag and head to the field so I wasn't left behind when the plane took off. I even decided to go to the game with Camden and the red lip emojis she sent after I'd sent a text letting her know meant she was happy to hear it.

There'd be no avoiding Silas anymore. Not now. Not after he'd… We'd have to talk at some point.

At the field, I dropped my bag with the person who would make sure it got on the bus. It was one small bag, so I would carry it on, though it was a chartered plane, so I didn't know that it mattered. Then I grabbed a bottle of water and headed to find Camden. She'd given me the section and seat number, but I didn't know this park. My pass hung around my neck, so none of the ushers even bothered to stop me.

"Found you," I said when I dropped into the seat next to her.

"You did. I would've sent out a search and rescue if you didn't show up soon." She nudged me with her shoulder.

Since the Knights were the visiting team, they'd already done their stretches and New York was on the field. Baseball did a body good. I was about to say just that when Camden said, "Watching these guys stretch sometimes makes me want to rethink the whole *no baseball players* thing."

"You know people think that way about your brothers."

She groaned and dropped her head back.

The sun was so bright that I kept my dark glasses on my nose and had my hair up in a bun. I'd also put about two tons of sunscreen on so that my sensitive skin wouldn't get burned. It was light and didn't do well in the sun.

"I don't need to be reminded of that," she said playfully.

"Why do you have the rule?" I twisted the cap off my water and took a big drink. It was already hot as balls outside and we had a few hours to be here. The Knights were batting first and the lead-off guy stepped out of the dugout. Silas usually batted fourth because at this point, he had the best batting average on the team. Brooks came up seventh, I thought.

Catchers weren't typically known for their bats, but Brooks was an exception.

"About not dating players?" she asked. I nodded, but she rolled her eyes. "It's a longish story, but the short version is that I don't want to end up with someone like my dad."

Now, I hadn't seen Mr. Briggs in a very long

time, but even when the guys had played in high school, he'd been a rough spectator to please.

"They aren't all like your dad."

She shook her head, her dark hair brushing against her shoulders. "Can't take the chance."

I wanted more information, but the game was starting and we were here to watch. Camden and I were seated in the second row from the field halfway between the dugout and home plate. It was a great spot and we had some protection from the nets in case someone tipped off and it came for us.

The first guy got on base. The second struck out. Then Jenner came up and when he saw us, he waved. Normally, most of the players stayed focused, but sometimes they'd wave or say *hi* to people they knew.

When Jenner went to the plate, Silas stepped out, putting his helmet on, but he noticed us so close and the corner of his mouth turned up like he had a secret. I guess he kind of did, but the move heated my skin.

At least today I could blame it on the actual heat.

Jenner got on base too. That meant Silas had the opportunity to get two more RBIs and while

Jenner would want that for the team, it wasn't great for their bet.

It'd been hard not to watch him at the plate before he'd buried his face between my legs. Now… it was impossible.

"Why are you looking at him like you want to eat him up?"

That was a splash of cold water on all of the dirty thoughts going through my mind.

"I'm not," I said quickly.

Camden pursed her lips and dropped her head to the side, telling me she didn't believe me. "You wouldn't happen to know anything about Silas being late to the field today, would you?"

I furrowed my brows. "No. He was late?"

She shook her head. "Only a minute, but Brooks said he last saw him outside of your room at the hotel. Coincidence?"

"I didn't make him late." Or rather, I hoped that I hadn't. He'd had plenty of time to get from the hotel to the field.

"Riiiight." Camden took a drink of her pop then turned back to me like there wasn't a whole baseball game playing out in front of us. "Last we talked, you were going to be avoiding my brother.

Now you're here and he was at your room. Come on." She was begging.

I sighed. "Yes. He and Brooks were arguing in front of my room. I don't know what about, so don't ask me about that. Ask them."

"Right. But those idiots get into arguments all the time."

Another drink from my bottle slid down, cooling my suddenly dry throat, as I hoped Camden would move on to other topics.

She didn't. She waited, as if she knew the silence would wear me down.

"He was there, like I said. Arguing with Brooks, but I don't know what it was about. I could hear their voices, but not what they were saying."

She rolled her eyes. "As a person who has witnessed far too many of my brothers' arguments, it probably wasn't anything important."

Brothers did that. Jayce and I used to bicker sometimes, but I didn't know the dynamic with the Briggs family anymore. "It seemed intense."

"It's always intense. So what happened next?"

Camden slid in her seat so she was facing me more than the game, as if it weren't happening at all while I kept one eye on her and the other on the game. The Knights were doing well so far.

"Hello, Amity. What happened next? I'm invested over here."

After a giggle, I shook my head. There was so much she didn't know that she didn't really want me to tell her. "It… got weird."

Her brow furrowed. "Weird? Like good weird? I've always wanted you to get with one of my brothers and assumed it'd be Silas, though Urban and Cobb might be better choices."

I snorted at the idea of her telling Silas that. While he didn't seem to want to actually be with me in a real way, saying one of his brothers should've been wouldn't have ended well. "Why is that?"

She shrugged. "I don't know. They're mostly not as intense. Remember when Silas would lay into them when they joined the high school team?"

I nodded because I'd noticed everything Silas had done back then.

Who was I kidding? I noticed it all now.

"Anyway, did he at least kiss you? I never pegged Silas as a pussy who didn't go after something he wanted."

Oh, how right she seemed to be. "We kissed," I admitted, but even I heard there was something more than kissing in that statement.

Her eyes widened and her mouth dropped

open. "Did you do more than kiss?" She dropped her voice to a whisper. "Did you have sex?" I shook my head quickly. "Something. Did you go down on him? Did *he* go down on *you*?"

It had to have been the burning in my face when she'd gotten to the right option because she suddenly sat back and bit her lips together in surprise.

"That's… really gross because he's my brother, but who knew my brother was a giver?" She rolled her eyes. "I'm going to have to wash my brain out. I mean, I figured he would be, though I didn't think about it at all, but to do it without anything in return. Unless he got something in return?"

I laughed a full belly laugh. Camden was a little embarrassed given the way she was rambling and this was about her brother after all. "No. He said something about there being rules, like I'm going to file a sexual harassment complaint, and then left."

Her shoulders slumped. "I mean… why would he think you'd do that?"

"He didn't say it, but it was kind of out there. Anyway… I'm not, but it was clear nothing more is going to happen."

"I wouldn't be so sure." She said this as if she had some kind of inside information and I was about to ask when the Knights' batter, Madden, grunted at the plate. He'd been hit in the shoulder by a fastball.

Now I'd never been hit by a ninety-five-mile-an-hour fastball but could imagine it didn't feel good. New York had changed pitchers, so it wasn't their starter and Madden was the first batter for this pitcher. That usually meant either the pitcher had no control—but this pitcher was known for his control—or something else was going on.

Camden leaned over and said, "I heard that pitcher thought Madden was talking to his girl and they've been beefing since."

"Was he? Flirting?" Cheating wasn't unheard of in sports and, I assumed, that was part of the reason Camden was adamant she wouldn't date a player. I tried not to think about it because Silas was all I thought about when it came to men and I didn't want to think about what could happen if we were actually together.

She shook her head. "Not as far as I know. I overheard Mom telling Dad that Madden swears he wasn't."

That also explained Silas's overreaction to me being alone with the guy. But if he was worried about a teammate moving in on another player's girlfriend, why would that matter when it came to me? I wasn't Silas's girlfriend.

Nothing else happened while the Knights were batting, but the first one up for New York got a ball lobbed at him. I was sure it hurt, but it wasn't as hard as the first one. That was when the umpire issued a warning to both sides.

"Oh, shit," I muttered. "A beanball war?" Camden nodded.

Those sucked. It basically meant that a batter was going to get hit every rotation until the umpire started ejecting people.

And *shit*. Silas was up second next inning.

CHAPTER 11
AMITY

*A*gain, no one else was hit that rotation and the Knights were up again. First batter, no issue. When Silas walked to the plate, Camden grabbed my arm and squeezed. He had the best average on the team right now, which made him a perfect target.

First pitch… hit him in the ribs and it wasn't a slower ball.

That had to hurt.

Silas grunted and curled into himself for a second then turned to the pitcher. He yelled, but I couldn't make out what he said. The pitcher threw his hands in the air as he shrugged and yelled something back.

One thing I knew was that baseball players could be brutal with their smack talk. Silas dropped his bat but didn't start for first base the way he should have. Instead, he took a step toward the mound.

"That's not good," I said to Camden. She shook her head.

Everything happened quickly after that and suddenly, Silas charged the mound. Soon, the benches cleared.

Base brawls didn't happen often, but when they did, they were massive. The bullpen ran out and joined, but I noticed Brooks with his hand on Cobb's chest holding him back. Cobb wasn't playing, but that didn't mean he wouldn't participate, but Brooks would do everything to keep that from happening.

If Cobb threw a punch even slightly off, it could end his career. Because he was a pitcher, he wouldn't necessarily come back from a small injury like Silas or Brooks would.

The umps and coaches—and I mean, *all* of the coaches—got it broken up pretty quickly, but Silas and the pitcher were ejected from the game.

"I wonder what that pitcher said to him," Camden said once we'd sat back down. "He's usually good at keeping his cool. I wonder if he'll tell me."

"Might want to wait until he calms down," I advised.

"Yeah, you wouldn't want her boyfriend to come after you the way he did the pitcher," a voice said from behind us. We both turned to find a twenty-five-ish-year-old woman with her blonde hair up in a ponytail and a beer in her hand.

"Silas isn't my boyfriend."

The redhead next to her leaned over. "We heard some of what you said. You might want to be careful where you go bragging."

I opened my mouth to counter, but Camden pulled me to my feet and pushed my back until I started walking. We climbed the stairs, but when we got to the concourse, I asked, "What was that about?"

"You can't argue with drunk women at a baseball game. First, it won't matter. Second, you work for the team."

Both were true, so I nodded. "Thanks."

"Why don't you check on Silas? I'm going to get my bag and head to the airport a little early. Grab some food. I'll see you back in Michigan." She reached over to hug me. At first, I froze but then quickly responded.

I wasn't much of a hugger. It always felt too close, I guess, and since I'd mostly hung around my brother and his friends in high school and my girlfriends and I hadn't been close, I'd never seen the appeal. But Camden's hug was reassuring and strong.

That was when I decided I liked hugging, even if it wasn't with a boyfriend.

Once she'd walked away, I headed down to the clubhouse to check on Silas. He'd get a verbal beatdown from the manager after the game, but right now, the guy was still managing the team. Silas would likely be alone in the clubhouse, though others might've gotten thrown from the game as well. It happened.

When I knocked gently and opened the door, he was alone, as far as I could tell. I let that door latch shut before making my way over to him.

Silas was in the chair in front of his locker staring ahead with so much intensity that it was possible he hadn't heard me come in. It wasn't until I was standing in front of him that he acknowledged my presence.

His hair was a little messy from his hat and

helmet, but it was sexy as hell. His shirt was untucked, but he hadn't showered yet or changed his clothes.

"You all right?"

His dark eyes lifted until they met mine. "I'm good."

"That ball looked like it hurt."

"Like a bitch," he said, but he didn't give me anything else about pain. "I'm pissed I got ejected."

I snorted. "You knew you were getting ejected the minute you dropped your bat."

A smile played at the corners of his lips. "Yeah. I guess I did."

"Let me see."

He knew I was talking about the spot where the ball had hit him, but I waved my hand to hurry him up.

As Silas stood, I had to take a step back so that his body didn't make contact with mine. He was too close; the heat radiating off his skin had mine melting. Instead of lifting his shirt, he just held his arm up, which meant I'd be doing the work.

I pulled the shirt up his body, revealing hard muscle covered by golden skin until I got to the purple mark about the size of a baseball.

"It's already starting to bruise," I told him.

"The ball was moving ninety miles an hour," he countered.

"Yeah." Which meant the pitcher had intended to hurt him. A beanball war could be raged with much slower pitches if they were just making a point. "I'm sorry you got it."

He shrugged and sat back down. "I'm not. That fucker got thrown too and the umps put out a final warning, so I bet no one else gets hit."

I furrowed my brows. "You planned that?" He didn't answer, but the hint of a smile crossed his face. "You're insane."

"No. It's done. It needed to be done." After wetting his lips, he asked, "Why aren't you still watching the game?"

"A couple of bitchy girls behind us overheard Camden and me talking. It wasn't going to be fruitful, so we left. She's headed to the airport."

"So do I want to know what they were bitchy about?"

"No." I told him quickly because the last thing I wanted to admit was that I'd told his sister what had happened in my hotel room before the game. "Just bitchy stuff." After an uncomfortable few minutes, I asked, "Are we alone in here?"

"Yeah. No one else from our team got thrown

that I know of, but if they did, they aren't in here. I was just going to shower. Want to join me?"

My cheeks heated. Of course I wasn't going to get into a shower with him in a visiting clubhouse. Anyone could walk in. I'd be fired for sure. It wasn't a serious question. "No, but that does bring up an interesting topic."

"Which is?" Again, his dark eyes threatened to melt me on the spot.

"You know what it is."

"Why don't you tell me so I'm sure?"

I took a deep breath to calm my nerves and, hopefully, my erratically beating heart. "Before the game… in my hotel room…"

"Come here."

Silas took my hand to lead me out into the hallway then into another room that looked like a therapy room, but it was empty. There was a table in the middle of the room and several desks.

"What are we doing here?" I asked as he lifted me onto the therapy table in the middle of the room, making me almost the same height but not quite.

He answered with his mouth. His hot breath feathered across me quickly before his lips crashed into mine. His mouth was demanding, almost brutal against mine, but no matter how hard he went, I wanted more.

This wasn't going to be some slow act that we both took our time with and I had no idea at what point he'd put it to an end, but I was here for as long as this lasted.

Silas pulled the straps of my sundress down then quickly snapped off my bra, exposing my breasts to the warm air and his touch. He cupped one as his tongue pushed past my lips.

I was ready for whatever he wanted to give.

"I need you," he said against my mouth and it sounded like part demand and part confession.

He wanted me. The evidence of that was pressing between my legs, touching the exact right spot. But he'd said he needed me. Part of me considered that maybe he was using me to work off his aggression from earlier.

At this point, I didn't care.

Silas yanked my panties down my legs and pushed my thighs apart. I was aching for him. Had been aching for him since we were in my hotel room. Then he yanked his shirt open, giving me access to all that hard muscle and the purple bruise that had deepened since I'd seen it minutes before.

He returned to kissing me as he undid his belt and baseball pants.

"Are you on the pill?" he asked, sounding as breathless as I felt.

I swallowed hard, unsure I was going to be able to speak. "An IUD."

His mouth claimed mine again, and at the same time, he shoved all the way inside me in one move, causing my breath to catch and my head to fall back.

It was a little uncomfortable at first as I got used to his size, but I was wet enough that it didn't hurt. Silas trailed kisses down my chest then took a nipple into his mouth and sucked right to the point before I would've said it was too much.

Silas was an expert at pushing right to the edge without going over.

Everything was exactly how it should've been, and I knew that Silas wouldn't hurt me. Whether because he cared about me or because of his loyalty to my brother, he wasn't going to physically hurt me.

My heart might've been another story.

He used one arm to support me as my arms began to fail to hold me up then used the other thumb to rub circles around my clit. He used exactly the right pressure, giving me what I needed to push me over the edge. He quickened his pace and followed after me.

I was going to have to do some clean up. Having sex with him without a condom wasn't the smartest decision of my life but I should've been covered and I couldn't help it.

With Silas, I didn't always make the best decisions.

Once he'd stopped thrusting, he held me to him as he slowly pulled out of me. I wasn't going to think about the mess on the table, but it was like he could hear my thoughts.

"I'll take care of it," he said quietly.

Finally, I lifted my eyelids him watching me with a newfound gentleness. Almost reverence. All of the hardness from earlier was gone.

"I…" Didn't know what to say or what this meant.

Was this the start of something? Was it a release of energy? Either way, I was fine with it. I'd wanted him for so long, I wouldn't have turned him down no matter the reason.

"Yeah." Silas still had his body between my legs and his hands rested on the table beside my hips.

He waited another moment before he pulled back and tucked himself back into his pants.

I hopped off the table and grabbed my panties from the ground and pulled them up. Then I got my bra and put that back on. We were silent during this time, but Silas stood back watching me and his eyes on me had me turning into a puddle.

There was no denying that I'd been in love with this man since I'd been a teenager and had accepted that it would only ever be one-sided. I wasn't going to let myself get lost in all of this. It was just sex.

Once I was put back together, I said, "What about those rules you mentioned earlier?"

He grinned. "I guess I decided to say *fuck the rules*."

I snorted. The rules weren't the only thing he'd fucked. Yeah, this might've been quick, but it'd been one of the hottest experiences of my life. Maybe that was partly because we were in a clubhouse, which was really a bad idea and anyone could've caught us. It was all kinds of forbidden that way.

"Yeah, but there *are* rules…"

He moved closer to me now that we were both dressed again. "We'll talk when we get back to

Michigan, but I think if we couldn't go one day since I said that…"

"True." I looked up at him. "To be clear, this isn't why I came to the clubhouse. I just wanted to check on you."

"I know. Because you're a nice person. So much better than I deserve."

I frowned. "Why do you say that?"

His jaw tightened and he shook his head. "We need to get out of here." He grabbed a rag and a bottle of cleaner, sprayed the table, then wiped it off so that all evidence of what we'd done was gone. Then he moved to the door and paused. This was my opportunity to give him an out.

"This can be a one-time thing, Silas." I swallowed hard. It wasn't what I wanted, but I also didn't want him to think it had to be more if he didn't want it to be. "You don't have to stress about it."

He turned and pushed his hand into my hair. "You think that now that I've had a taste of you that I can just go back?" He shook his head and my stomach dropped with the excitement of a roller-coaster. "I can't do that, Amity. Even though it makes me a selfish bastard, I can't go back."

Before I could ask for clarification, his lips

pressed against mine again and soon we were back to the on ramp of what we'd just done. His tongue on mine reminded me of what it could do and I was about ready to start undressing him, but he had the sense to bring it to an end as soon as my hands went to his belt.

"No time," he said with regret. Then he licked his bottom lip. "When we get home…"

"Right." I shook my head to clear all of the naughty thoughts going through it. "When we get home."

Now I had a whole-ass plane ride to worry about whether or not he was going to change his mind. Silas could get spooked in those couple of hours, but the fact that I felt his gaze on me the entire trip made me suspect that wasn't going to happen.

It was like the sky had opened up to let the sun shine down because Silas Briggs was finally mine.

CHAPTER 12
SILAS

The fucking rules meant that I had to be with the team until we were released back home. We'd played the day game in New York. I'd fucked Amity quickly in a clubhouse. Now I was expected to wait until who-knew-when to be with her again. All because I had to take team transportation—which she was on, too—then have a team meeting when we got back to our own clubhouse while she could leave.

Or I assumed she could. She was staff and while she had to take transportation to and from the away games with us and be at the hotel at night like we did, she didn't have to stick around for any meetings. I didn't think.

Fuck. I guess I didn't really know.

We all filed off the bus back in Kalamazoo, but Amity hurried off like her ass was on fire. At least she went into the stadium. I was headed there, but Camden was leaning on the side of the building waiting for something, and I had to assume it was Brooks or me.

"What's up?" I asked when I got close enough.

"I want you and Brooks to come to dinner at Mom and Dad's with me tonight."

"No." I had other, more important, and much more fun, plans.

She sighed. "Brooks already said he'd come and I'm going to ask Amity to come too, so you may as well be there. It'll be the only way you can spend time with her."

My eyes narrowed on my little sister. "What do you know?"

She groaned and rubbed a finger up and down between her eyebrows. "More than I should, but I guess I'm glad you're a giver."

I snorted. Knowing anything like that about me probably made Camden want to dry heave into an empty bucket. It would me if the situation were reversed.

I couldn't explain it, but knowing stuff my brothers did had no effect. Even considering that my baby sister let someone touch her—even though I knew she had—made me want to break off the dicks of every guy around me.

"She's not going to say *yes*," I told her because stupidly, I'd thought our plans for the night were already known to both of us.

Camden held up her phone and waved it close to my face. "She already said she'd be there. She just has to go home to shower first." The small shiver that crossed her body made me wonder how much of what Amity and I had done she knew. As in did she know it was at a point that Amity wouldn't have been able to shower after?

Well… fuck. I guess that meant I was going to dinner at my parents' house because if that was where Amity was going to be, that was where I would be, too.

"Fine," I said with a sigh. "I'll be there at seven." Because I knew that was usually when Mom and Dad had dinner. They had a cook to make it for them, but dinner was always at seven.

Camden gave me a satisfied grin, as if she'd known I would agree to it before she'd asked. Getting Amity there was a good way to get me, too. My sister was smart, but she didn't always use her brains for good.

Dinner at my parents was usually fine. Sometimes stressful if Dad decided to talk about our careers.

It wasn't good enough that he'd raised four Major League baseball players. No. He wanted to guide our careers to the Hall of Fame so that his baseball dynasty would be realized. *Fuck.* We just wanted to play.

I dropped into a chair in the room where we were having our post-road-trip meeting, then Jenner dropped beside me and Brooks beside him. There were rows of tables and chairs to accommodate the entire team.

Jenner shook his head before he spoke. "What's going on with you?"

I furrowed my brows. "I don't know what you mean." For the most part, I was playing great. I'd been inside Amity just hours ago. As far as I could tell, there wasn't a damn thing wrong with me.

I mean… I had gotten kicked out of the game, so there was that, and I expected a little hell for that.

Jenner frowned. "You shouldn't be playing so well."

Thankfully, the meeting hadn't started because I

let out a full laugh. "What the fuck's that supposed to mean?"

"Amity being here should be fucking with your head. Don't try to deny that you have a thing for her, but I thought for sure it'd be fucking with your head. I thought that maybe the second game it was finally kicking in, but no. What gives?"

I furrowed my brows and looked over at him. "You want Amity to fuck with my game? Do you hate winning?"

Brooks leaned forward. "Sounds like he hates winning."

"That's what I'm thinking."

My brother chuckled then sat back and folded his arms over his chest.

"No," Jenner said. "I fucking love winning, which is why I wanted her to fuck with you so I could win the bet."

From the other side of him, Brooks muttered, "Jesus Christ."

But me... I didn't say anything and kept my gaze forward, willing this damn meeting to start. I wasn't about to give Jenner shit.

"Oh, really?" The sound of his voice was far too self-satisfied.

Not telling him anything had told him everything.

Luckily, our manager came in to talk to us about the team we were playing tomorrow and anything he had to say about how we'd just played.

I wouldn't have to sit through a lecture about getting kicked out of the game. I'd gotten that in New York. Now that it was done, it was done. He wouldn't bring it up again. He'd understood why I'd done it and was actually grateful to end to the bean-ball war. It helped that we'd still won.

In the end, an hour later, I was able to haul ass out of there and get home to change for dinner at my parents'.

Just before seven, I arrived at their house. Camden and Brooks were already there, but I didn't see Amity yet. I wasn't going to ask.

The less my family knew, the better. At least for now.

Mom gave me a hug and Dad shook my hand. Both started talking about the series with New York while Dad made drinks. I didn't want one.

Then the knock came and Camden ran to the door. She came back with Amity.

Fuck, that woman was beautiful.

Her auburn hair was cascading down over her

shoulders and she was wearing another sundress. I fucking loved sundress season with her around. The skirt brushed against her thighs, leaving the rest of her legs for me to feast on. Though she wasn't very tall, which meant not as much skin as if she'd been naked.

Everyone greeted her, but Mom hurried over and pulled Amity into her arms.

"I'm so glad you're back in town," Mom said to her. Mom had always loved Amity and seeing her at games when I'd been in school. I thought she hoped that she and Camden would be better friends than they had been. Which meant Mom was now getting her wish. Camden and Amity were better friends than I would've liked, given that my sister now knew some of what had happened between us.

"Thank you. I'm glad to be back." Amity's cheeks pinked up just enough for me to notice when her gaze found mine. No one else would have noticed.

Fuck. I wanted to kiss her, but here in front of my family would've been too soon. Thankfully, it was time for dinner. While everyone else filed out, I hung back until Amity got close enough for me to reach out to.

I brushed hair off of one shoulder and trailed

my fingertips over it and down her back until my hand settled right above her ass.

"How did she get you here?" I asked her quietly as we made our way toward the dining room.

"Camden said you were going to be here and wanted me to be, too." She leaned back to look up at me. "Did you not want me here?"

"Fuck, *I* don't even want to be here." I pinched her chin between my thumb and forefinger to tilt her head up toward me. "I'd much rather be somewhere else doing something very different."

Her face flushed a gorgeous pink, which was so unlike Amity. She'd grown up around a bunch of guys, many of whom had become professional athletes. Embarrassment wasn't something she did very often and I didn't even think this *was* embarrassment. But if I could make this woman blush at all, it would be my life's mission to continue trying to make it happen.

I leaned down and gently pressed my lips to hers. However, it didn't get as far as I'd wanted because my father cleared his throat.

"We're waiting for the two of you," he said curtly.

Amity pulled back quickly then hurried into the

dining room while my father, looking like an older version of us guys, stood there giving me the stare-down.

That shit didn't work on any of us anymore and it pissed him right off.

I took the open seat across from Amity since Camden was already sitting right beside her and there wasn't another chair on the other side. Instead, I got stuck next to Brooks with our parents on the ends.

"Amity, I was so excited to see that you'd been hired by the team," Mom told her. "It's been too long since we've seen you."

Dad snorted, which caught Mom's attention and made her furrow her brows.

Mom wasn't going to put up with any shit from Dad about Amity being around. Neither would I. Didn't matter if they knew my feelings or not.

"Thank you, Mrs. Briggs. I'm very happy to be a part of it." Her gray gaze flitted over me then focused on her plate.

"Well, glad I'm not the only Briggs happy to have some more estrogen in the place," Camden added, then she bumped Amity's shoulder with her own. "Creates a little more balance."

"The last thing we need is more women around here," Dad countered, tensing my jaw.

"I disagree," Camden countered.

She'd never backed down from Dad once in her life. We guys didn't, either, but we'd learned over the years that some battles weren't worth the fight and we'd let him think whatever he'd wanted while we'd done whatever we'd wanted.

Camden had not learned that lesson.

"You can have your little friends outside of the house," Dad told her. "Inside, we need to remain focused. The last thing your brothers need is to get caught up in some woman."

Amity pinched her lips together between her teeth. *Too late, Pops.* I was already caught up over this woman. She just didn't know it yet.

"OK, well," Camden continued, "maybe teach your sons how to control themselves so they don't act like horny little freaks just because a woman comes around."

"Jesus Christ, Camden." I sat back in my chair while Brooks added, "What the fuck?"

Camden snickered because she knew we'd never not controlled ourselves and that had nothing to do with what our father was saying. Just fucking why did he have to be saying it in front of Amity? She looked so fucking uncomfortable and I opened my mouth to shut him down when my mother beat me to it.

"Conrad, we have a guest and I think maybe we could keep things lighter." Mom gave Dad a poignant look. Even he listened to Mom most of the time because he knew if she was stepping in, he was going too far.

The conversation changed, but the air was still tense. As soon as we'd finished eating, though, Amity, who had set her fork down soon after Dad's little rant, cleared her throat.

"Thank you for dinner, Mrs. Briggs. Mr. Briggs. I think I'm going to head home."

"Seriously?" Camden asked, not trying to hide her disappointment. She probably wanted Amity to spend a few hours here. *Fuck.* Brooks and I weren't even going to do that. We had a game tomorrow.

"Yeah, I'm sorry. I'm really tired from the game then the trip." She glanced at me quickly. There were a couple of other reasons I could think of that she would've been tired and it took everything to keep from grinning at her.

Amity pushed from the table and Mom stood at the same time.

"Well, we were very happy to have you, Amity."

Mom said, but Dad grunted. "We hope to see more of you now that you're back in town."

Dad, the fucking asshole, said nothing, but when Amity turned to walk out of the dining room, I hopped up to follow her.

"Are you really going home?" I asked, making her turn back toward me.

"I am. I was serious when I said I was tired." The corners of her eyes sagged slightly, which meant she was telling the truth. "I'm not used to traveling the way the team does. I'll get used to it, but this was a first for me."

I ran my palms down her arms until I could take her hands in mine. "I'll take you."

"I have my car," she countered. "Really. I'm going to go home and go to bed."

"Sounds good to me." I took another step toward her and leaned in close so that no one trying to hear what was being said could. "We should probably talk."

She nodded, but something about her movements said she was nervous. "But we don't have to tonight. Seriously. Stay with your family."

I pushed my fingers into her hair and ran my thumb over her cheek. "Good night, then." I leaned in and kissed her. And I didn't give a fuck who saw it.

Amity melted into me and wrapped one arm around my shoulder and threaded her fingers into the hair at the back of my neck. When I pulled her against me, I fully intended to follow her ass home, but when she pulled back, I saw how tired she was again and knew I couldn't do that. I could kiss her quickly one more time and that, I did do.

And I may have watched her walk to her car in the driveway while fighting the urge to follow her again.

The last thing I wanted to do was stay with my family. I also wasn't going to push Amity harder than I already had. She probably had to get her thoughts together as much as I did but I knew what I wanted and wouldn't stop unless she told me to.

Two hours later, I was on the verge of cutting Dad off if Brooks hadn't beaten me to it. He was going on and on about our careers, which were going fucking fantastic, but it still wasn't enough for him. We were all in the living room. Camden was on her phone doing her best to ignore what was going on when her phone rang in her hands, startling her.

She furrowed her brows. "It's Amity." Now *that* brought all of my attention right to my sister. "Hello?" She listened intently, but her gaze jumped to mine. "You're OK, right?"

My stomach plummeted.

"Yeah. Of course. I'll be there in, like, fifteen minutes." Then she ended the call.

I was already on my feet. "What's going on?"

She still looked confused when she answered, "Amity had a car accident." And that was when I wanted to puke. Memories of the night her brother had died flooded through me, causing my blood to run cold. Clearly, Amity had called. She wasn't dead, but I needed to see that for myself. "She's OK. She doesn't have her car and there was something about her dad insisting she have someone take her home and not call an Uber."

"Fuck an Uber. I'm going to get her."

"Silas." She reached out and grabbed my arm to stop me. "She called *me*."

That, I knew and I wanted to know why, but for now, I needed to see Amity and make sure she was really OK. We didn't have the best history with car accidents and fuck, all I could picture in my head was her dead brother leaning against the steering wheel of my car.

"I'm going, Camden. You stay here or go home. I don't care. I'm going."

I didn't wait for an answer because if I didn't get my eyes on Amity soon, I was going to lose my fucking mind.

CHAPTER 13
AMITY

Silas's dad had always been a lot. Singularly focused on the boys having the careers he wanted them to have. They were all great athletes, but it still didn't seem to be enough for Mr. Briggs.

Maybe I'd been distracted. I didn't think so because the car had come out of nowhere and slammed into the passenger side of my car then pushed me to the other side of the road. I hadn't been going very fast and I knew for a fact that the light had been green when I'd gone through.

"Are you OK?" someone asked as I sat, stunned, in my car.

I glanced over and said, "I think so" before getting out of my car. After taking a quick inventory of my body, I decided I was going to be sore tomorrow, but overall, nothing hurt too much. Was that just the adrenaline? I didn't think so, but I also didn't know.

The police arrived almost immediately. Apparently, a car had been just behind me and the driver had seen the whole thing.

The officer asked if I wanted an ambulance and I told him I wasn't sure but didn't think so. He took my statement then went over to the driver of the other car.

More police arrived and an ambulance, but I didn't know for whom. I was fine.

While I waited, I pulled my phone out of my pocket. I needed to hear my dad's voice. That deep tenor would help sooth my nerves. This had been a minor accident, but car accidents freaked me out because of how my brother had died. His should've been a minor accident, too.

"How was your first trip with the team?" Dad asked instead of saying *hello*. Most of the time, he acted like we were already in the middle of a conversation when he answered. It was almost never with *hello*.

"It went well," I told him.

He immediately responded, "What's wrong,

Amity? I can hear it in your voice. What happened on the trip?"

I swallowed hard. "It wasn't the trip. I just had a car accident."

"What? Are you OK? What happened?" What sounded like a chair hitting the wall startled me. It was like he'd stood up quickly and sent the chair into the wall.

"I'm OK, Dad. It's not a big accident. Someone ran a red light." I glanced at the caved-in side of my car. "My car might be dead, though."

"I don't care about the car, Amity. I care about you. Are you at the hospital?"

"No. I think I'm all right."

"You're getting checked out. Go to the hospital." That was definitely an order, and I wasn't going to protest. It'd make both of us feel better.

"There's an ambulance here, but they haven't taken anyone, so I think everyone's fine, but I'll tell them I need to be checked out."

"Call me when you're done."

After agreeing, I hung up. Dad was at an away game with his own baseball team. They were high school, sure, but they traveled all over the state in their division. I wasn't sure where exactly he was, but it wasn't here, so he couldn't meet me.

I did what I'd promised. I went to the paramedic and told the tall, blonde woman that I wanted to get checked out at the hospital. When she went into high alert, I explained that I thought I was fine, but that my brother had died in a car accident and my dad had insisted. She understood and loaded me up.

Two hours later, I was sitting on the end of the gurney in the emergency department calling my dad again.

"Everything's fine," I told him before he could even answer. "The doctor said there are no signs of concussion, though I didn't hit my head, so I wasn't worried. Everything else checked out fine as well. They did x-rays to be sure. I'm good."

A relieved breath blew against the phone. "I'm very glad to hear that." Dad had been finishing a game when I'd called him or close to finishing, anyway. "You'll need to get some rest. Maybe take tomorrow off."

"I will if I need to." That was all the promise he was going to get. "I'm going to call an Uber to get home. My car had to be towed. I think I'll need a new one." Which sucked because I'd just gotten that one. At least I was fully insured and this wasn't going to break me financially.

"Cars can be replaced. Daughters can't be." His voice was dripping with sadness. Another reminder that both of us knew just how irreplaceable people were. We both missed my brother every single day. "Promise me you won't take an Uber. I'd come get you, but we're on the bus and it'll be another hour before I'm home. If I were in Kalamazoo, I'd already be there."

"I know, Dad. I know you would've shown up at the scene. I'll be fine."

"Amity."

I couldn't say *no* to him when he spoke to me with so much concern. I'd have to call someone for a ride.

"And don't stay alone tonight," he added. I was about to protest when he said, "Please just humor your old man."

Well, yeah. I couldn't argue with him there. After promising, I had to think of whom I could call. Camden was the only friend I was close enough with, and who lived in the city, to not only ask for a ride home, but to ask to spend the night because it'd make my father feel better.

She knew our history. She'd been around when Jayce had died and seen the relentless pain my family had gone through.

Camden would understand.

When I called her, she said she'd be here in fifteen minutes. There was no hesitation and for that, I was thankful.

But it wasn't Camden who walked through the door in the emergency department.

It was Silas. And he looked both angry and worried.

"What're you doing here?" I asked when he came through my door. I'd already been discharged, but they'd said I could wait back here instead of the waiting room for my ride.

He scowled. "I heard the phone call with my sister. When she said you'd been in an accident, I thought my heart was going to stop. Are you all right?" He came to a stop in front of me then ran his hands over my shoulders and down my arms.

Silas had been there the night my brother died, so I could see why someone else he knew being in an accident would cause him to worry. That night would haunt us all forever.

"Yeah. The doctor said everything checked out. I'll likely be sore and maybe bruised from the seatbelt a little but otherwise fine." I quickly wet my lips. "Is Camden in the car? Is she with you?"

His brows furrowed. "Is there a reason you'd prefer my sister over me?"

I shook my head. "I called her, that's all. I assumed she'd be here."

"I told her not to come."

Well, that changed everything, I supposed. No way could I ask Silas to spend the night. That would've been weird. After all, I didn't know if we were two friends who'd had sex at the stadium or what. Asking him to spend the night would've possibly been pushing into a territory I shouldn't.

Instead of telling him all of that, I hopped off the bed and headed out the door.

Silas took my hand as he led me to the car. Then he made sure I was in and shut my door before going over to his side. As he pulled away from the hospital, he asked, "So everything was fine?"

"Everything was fine. Except my car." I sighed because not having a car, even for a little while, was going to suck.

"Cars can be replaced."

I snorted. "That's what my dad said, but neither of you is the one who's going to be without a car for however long insurance takes to pay the loan so that I can get a new one."

His grip tightened on the steering wheel. "I will literally go out tomorrow and buy you a car."

Now I had to giggle. He had to know how ridiculous that sounded. Most people couldn't buy a car at the drop of a hat. I sure couldn't.

Silas got us to my apartment building and this was the first time he'd been here. I was sure it was much different than wherever he lived.

"Thanks for the ride," I told him as I put my hand on the handle of the door.

"Really?" He sat back and ran his index finger over his top lip. "Just 'thanks for the ride'?"

I sighed. "It's been kind of a long night, Silas. After listening to your father talk about how you boys should basically just fuck 'em and forget 'em, I had a car accident. Yes, it was minor, but it's definitely stirred up a bunch of memories for me. Probably for you, too." He didn't indicate one way or another yet I knew it was true.

"My dad can get fucked. I'm grown. He says shit and I, along with the rest of the guys, don't usually fight him on it because it's not fucking worth it. He wasn't talking about you."

I snorted. "He absolutely was talking about me. He saw you kiss me in the living room. Then unleashed that. He was talking about me."

"I don't care." He tapped the wheel with his hand to accentuate each word. I guess he didn't care. "How about we go into your apartment and talk about all of this?"

Though I didn't think it was a good idea, I got out of his car and led him to my one-bedroom apartment. I loved this place. It was an old-style building with exposed brick on one wall. I'd had it decorated with a very modern look, but it was absolutely lived in.

I pushed my shoes off at the door and he did the same because his mother had taught him manners. If someone took their shoes off when they entered their house, you did, too. It was an unwritten rule.

"Want a drink?" I asked.

"You sit down. I'll get them." He gave me a little nudge toward the living room. My apartment was open concept, so the living room, dining area, and kitchen were basically all one room.

"You don't know where anything is," I countered.

"It's a kitchen. I'm sure I can figure it out," he said. Well… yeah. I supposed so. I went to the couch and sat while he was in the kitchen. "What do you want to drink? No alcohol."

"I wasn't going to ask for any. A water would be good." There was no chance I'd take in a single drop of alcohol when I'd just had an accident. They hadn't seen a head injury, but what if…

Silas returned with two bottles of water, handed one off to me, then sat on the other end of the couch. Each of us had one leg propped up and our bodies turned so that we were facing each other.

"Why'd you call Camden?" he asked before I could say a word.

After sighing, I said, "My dad didn't want me to be alone tonight. She's the person I'm close enough to that I can ask."

"To spend the night?" He raised an eyebrow and I nodded. "Was that her going down on you at the hotel earlier today?"

I slapped a hand over my face, not believing he'd just said that. "No. Definitely not."

"Then I'd say you're pretty fucking close to me."

I rolled my eyes. "Doubtful. I'm sure you've done that with many, many women. It doesn't make me special."

His hand gripped the water bottle so hard that it crinkled. "You'd be wrong."

"On which part?" I countered. "Because I'm pretty sure—"

He cut me off. "That it doesn't make you special." There was no way that Silas hadn't fucked at least a quarter of Kalamazoo. I didn't care. We weren't together, but it made me sure that I was deluding myself on this whole thing. "You've always been special, Amity."

My heart thumped erratically. "So, you're going to spend the night to make sure I don't die in my sleep? Because that's what my dad is probably worried about."

He closed his eyes for a moment before opening them again. "I'm spending the night so you're not alone, but please don't paint any more visuals like that. I can't take that."

There was such a sincerity in his voice that I now felt bad for saying it in the first place.

"What does that mean? For us? Silas, I don't usually hook up with baseball players. Certainly not when doing my job and I—"

"The timing was bad, I'll admit." He set the water on the table. "But I've wanted you so fucking badly for so fucking long that it was like I couldn't wait another minute." My body tingled with heat at his words. "But yeah, I should've waited. Gotten you in a bed. Taken my time with you." He pushed his folded leg straight then tapped his thigh. "Come here."

I couldn't say *no* to the man if I wanted to. After putting my own bottle on the table, I crawled over to him and onto his lap, straddling his hips. He pushed his fingers into the hair on both sides of my face.

"You scared the fuck out of me tonight," he whispered.

"*I* didn't do it." The accident hadn't been my fault.

The corners of his lips turned up just slightly before he pulled my mouth to his. At first, Silas kissed me softly, as if I were made of glass and would break. But when I ground into his growing erection, he groaned and became more aggressive. He thrust his tongue into my mouth and I melted. I thought this would be going somewhere, but he brought the kiss to an end.

I pouted. I pouted the way a child who'd been told *no* to the ice cream she wanted would've. My pout made him snort.

"You were in an accident today. I'm not going to fuck you."

I cocked my head to the side. "I bet I could convince you."

"I bet you couldn't. What if you're hurt?"

"I'm not."

"Tell me something else that you want," he said instead. "Anything else."

I sighed and shrugged. "Cereal. I'm hungry."

His laughter followed us into the kitchen, where Silas set out a bowl for both of us and grabbed my favorite cereal, which wasn't something I'd bet he ever ate. It wasn't healthy at all. Then he brought the milk over.

I was already pouring my cereal when he poured the milk into his empty bowl. I set the box on the counter roughly.

"What kind of psycho puts the milk in the bowl first?" I asked, staring at him like he was in fact a certifiably crazy person.

"What do you mean? Lots of people." He poured the cereal into the bowl on top of the milk as I stared in horror.

"Uh… I bet not. How do you control the milk-to-cereal ratio?"

He snorted. "I can control how much cereal goes into the bowl."

Still, I looked at him as if his English weren't

making any sense to me. "I don't think I can trust a person who puts the milk in the bowl first."

Now he laughed loudly. "You need a better system on who to trust."

"I don't know. I'm rethinking everything."

His smile only grew wider. "You know we're going to have to tell my mother we're together."

My eyebrows shot sky high. "We're together?"

"Yeah, we are. But we knew each other before you started working for the team. This shouldn't be a problem and she likes you."

"I'm not sure she likes me that much," I muttered, but he heard me. "Besides, are you rushing into that decision? It means completely changing your lifestyle."

His brows furrowed and he stopped the spoon halfway to his mouth. "What are you talking about?"

"The women. The random hookups in bar bathrooms."

His jaw tightened. "I told you nothing happened with that woman."

I waved him off. "It's just an example. I know how you guys are. How you've always been. Girls threw themselves at you in high school and that hasn't changed. Unfortunately, I also know that you,

Jenner, and my brother took pretty much every opportunity that you got. That can be hard to change and I don't want you to change it if you don't want to. I also don't want to get hurt."

Because if Silas cheated on me, I'd never recover.

"Fuck whatever lifestyle you imagine I've been living," he told me, though I knew what that was. It wasn't my imagination. "My family, my job—they aren't going to keep me from what I want and I want you." He came closer and cupped my cheek. "I've always wanted you. I was just too stupid to go after you before."

Stupid or not, there were so many potential things that could go wrong in this situation.

Silas must've seen my hesitation because then he said, "I'll prove it."

CHAPTER 14
SILAS

I'd prove it to Amity.

I'd said those words and I meant them. I'd prove to her that nothing about my life was going to stand in the way of having her. She was more important than all of that put together. Even if the truth about her brother's accident would've likely ruined it all. There was no reason to think she'd ever find out.

Her father had promised me when it had happened that he wouldn't tell her. I'd thought he would've hated me and put the blame on me, but he hadn't. And he'd never told her that the accident had been my fault. If she ever found out, it would mean I'd never have her in my life again.

It had broken my fucking heart watching her

grieve her brother knowing that if not for me, he would've still been alive. That was part of the reason I pushed myself so hard in the game.

I was playing for both of us.

It didn't matter if it'd been seven years.

Amity looked up at me with those big, gray eyes. I'd never seen eyes quite the color of hers and couldn't remember if her mom had that color. Her dad sure as hell didn't. He had brown eyes that could shoot the worst death stares if you were a member of his team not doing what he should have been doing.

Hers were fucking beautiful.

"I'm going to go to bed," she said quietly. "Do you…?" She looked away and wet her lips as if what she was going to ask were hard for her. "Do you want to sleep in the bedroom with me or on the couch?"

How this woman didn't already know the answer to that question, I had no idea. The only thing that would keep me from her bed was her.

"With you," I told her, then I leaned in to kiss her again. *Fuck.* I really wished she hadn't had an accident tonight. For many reasons, but wanting her more than I'd ever wanted anyone was at the top of the list. Right after her not being hurt. I moved away from her and grabbed her bowl. "You go ahead. I'll clean this up." Though she hadn't eaten much of her snack. If she got hungry later, I'd get her one. "I'll just be a minute."

She nodded then headed toward what I assumed was the bedroom. I hadn't been here before, but it was the only place that led to another room.

After grabbing her bowl, I stacked it with mine and went to the sink intending to empty them and rinse the bowls. But when she pulled her shirt over her head before she got into the bedroom, I knew that I wasn't going to be rinsing anything and wondered if this was part of her convincing me, as she'd said earlier she intended to do.

Instead, I left the bowls, locked the door, and turned off all the lights on my way to her bedroom. I'd have to go by home in the morning to change and shower and brush my teeth. It'd have to be early, too, because we started early the next day, but tonight… I didn't give a shit about any of that.

When I got to Amity's room, I noticed that it looked about how I would've pictured it if anyone had told me to picture Amity's bedroom. It was modern and clean. Not too girly, but with a feminine touch. Basically, it was Amity.

She had curtains on the window, but they were just enough to block anyone's view. They definitely weren't the blackout curtains that hung in my bedroom. At least this way, I wouldn't oversleep.

It was Amity who made me stop. She was in her bed, under the blanket with her arms on top of it. Her shoulders were bare, which had me guessing that the rest of her was too.

Fuck. She slept naked. Or at least she was tonight and now I had no doubt that this was part of her trying to convince me to fuck her.

It'd been hard to say *no* when she'd been fully clothed. I didn't know that I'd be able to with her naked.

I pulled off my T-shirt and pushed down my jeans with the intention of sleeping in my boxer briefs. Then I climbed in beside her. She turned onto her side to face me with a little mischievous grin on her face.

"You know you don't actually have to spend the night, right?" she asked. As if I'd only be here because I had to be.

Instead of telling her that, I showed her.

I brushed her hair over her shoulder then leaned in to kiss her.

It was only meant to be a goodnight kiss.

Simple. But getting my lips on Amity… my desire overrode all of the sensible things my brain was reminding me.

Amity pushed her body into mine. When I reached beneath the comforter to wrap my arm around her waist, I found out she was indeed naked beneath. That was when the final strings of willpower completely vanished.

Her fingers skated down my chest, hesitating when she got to my lower abdomen, but only for a moment before she slipped her hand into my boxers. She pushed against the head of my cock and I would've sworn I was about to blow it right then.

I'd wanted this woman for so long… Sure. We'd had a quick fuck in the clubhouse in New York earlier that day, but it felt like too long ago.

When she wrapped those fingers around my cock, I had to pull back.

"Amity…" Her name came out like a warning. "You were in an accident tonight."

"I told you, I'm fine. Doctors agree." She stroked me once for effect and it was everything I could do not to roll my damn eyes back in my head. That felt better than anyone's hand ever had. "Why don't you trust me to know what I can do or what I can't?" That was a good point. "Besides," she added quietly, "it wasn't bad and I want to remember that I'm alive."

Which meant memories of her brother had been reminding her of what could have happened, just like they had me.

Well, fuck. That, I couldn't say *no* to.

So I rolled on my back in a way that made sure she wouldn't lose her grip on me and pushed my boxers down so they could get lost somewhere beneath the covers. Then I laid back with my hands behind my head, giving her the go ahead to do whatever it was she set out to do.

Amity wet her lips, making me swallow hard, then pushed the blanket back so she could see where she was touching me. After she propped herself up on her elbow, she stroked me several times, watching her hand move along my cock. Then she rose onto her knees, leaned over, and took me into her mouth.

My hands refused to stay behind my head then.

This beautiful, naked woman had my cock in her mouth. I couldn't blame my hands for needing to touch her.

First, I settled my hand on her lower back then slid up until my fingers could fist in her hair. She groaned, so I tightened my hold on her. She shivered. *Fuck.* She liked her hair pulled a little. That, I could do.

As if I were the one controlling the pace, I pushed her head down then squeezed her hair to bring it back up. Her tongue slid along the entire length of my cock before she cupped my balls.

I didn't want to know why she was so fucking good at this, but if she didn't stop soon… it was going to end.

This time, when she went to slide down, I kept my hold on her hair so she couldn't. That gray gaze, burning with desire, met mine.

"Unless you want this to be the end, you have to stop."

The corners of her mouth turned up in a devilish grin. "Wouldn't want that, now, would I?"

I chuckled quietly then quickly got her on her back. I used my fingers and my mouth to make sure she was as wet as she could be.

The sounds coming from Amity had me wanting to cum before I even got inside her. They were quiet and sweet and I could tell they weren't faked. She wasn't trying to sound like a porn star. She was just… her.

When I pushed inside her, her head fell back

and she groaned. She dug her nails into my shoulders as I pulled out and then back in. Her knees squeezed my sides, so I pushed one up as far as it would toward her tits. This gave me more room and hit her at a different angle. Then I did the same with the other so I could go deeper. No matter how deep I got, it wasn't enough. I wanted more.

Amity made no move to change our positions and I wasn't going to, either. If she wanted to be a pillow princess tonight and just lie there to take me, I was fine with that.

I pulled back so I could see where we were connected and watched myself disappear inside her pussy. That was all it took.

I exploded like a fucking rocket inside her.

Fuck. She hadn't had an orgasm yet. I could fix that.

Once the pleasure had left my body, I pushed her legs open wide and descended. I licked her hard clit and sucked it between my teeth while massaging her inner thighs.

That was all it took. Her muscles tightened and those sounds got a little louder as I gave her the pleasure she gave me. When her body relaxed, I gently brought her legs together again.

"Damn," she said, sounding out of breath, as if

she'd just been for a run. She hadn't been. I'd done that.

"Yeah. Damn."

There weren't any other words to describe it.

Amity used the bathroom first then came back and snuggled down in the bed to wait for me. I got myself cleaned up quickly before climbing into bed and pulling her to me.

The feel of her skin against me was fucking magical.

"Do I need to be worried?" Amity asked as I held her close to my chest.

"About?"

"We haven't used a condom…"

Oh, right. I was the manwhore. While her assumption about my life wasn't completely accurate, it wasn't completely inaccurate, either. "You don't need to be worried," I told her.

"No?" she asked, as if she might not believe me.

"I've never been with anyone without a condom that I provided," I told her. "Until you."

She pushed up to lean on her elbow so she could see me. "Really?"

I shook my head. "Do you think I'd risk getting some random woman pregnant? Not to mention the other host of things that could come from it. Fuck no."

"But you're not worried about getting me pregnant? Or me giving you anything?"

Did I want a kid right now? Fuck no. If it did accidentally happen with Amity? I'd be all in because I already was.

"No," I told her. "You're on birth control. Unlikely to get pregnant, right?" She nodded. "You're a careful person, Amity. I trust you were careful before me and I trust you to be careful with me." More than I'd ever trusted anyone in my life.

"I've never not used a condom," she told me and my stomach clenched. I didn't really want to know, if I were being honest. "You're right. I'm as careful as they come."

"Then we don't need to talk about it, right?" Because hearing about her with other men wasn't something I could handle.

"Right." She slid back in beside me. "And I trust you," she added. "I even trust you to get me a cookie because I'm still hungry since I didn't finish my cereal."

I chuckled but still fished around under the blanket to find my boxer briefs and swung my legs over the side. I pulled them up as I stood. If my woman wanted a cookie, I was getting her a damn cookie.

It only took a minute, but I was back with a plate of three cookies and a small glass of milk. She sat up, tucking the blanket under her arms as if I hadn't already seen everything she was hiding under the blanket. But, hey, if this made her feel more comfortable, I wasn't going to say a thing.

"Want one?" she asked, offering me a cookie.

I shook my head as I said, "Game tomorrow. I already had cereal."

She furrowed her brows. "You had two bites."

"Two bites too many of that sugary shit."

I was an athlete. Sure. Sometimes I could go off-track, but the vast majority of the time, I ate the way I was supposed to. You couldn't stay in peak physical shape while eating sugary cereal and cookies more than occasionally.

"You're missing out." She took a big bite of the chocolate chip cookie then smiled.

She definitely made that cookie look good.

I leaned against the headboard as she ate. We talked about the fight in New York and the fact that while she thought it was hot, she didn't like seeing me fight. It was good it didn't happen too often, but for that game, it needed to. If I hadn't gone after the pitcher when I had, the next person would've been hit, too. That beanball game would've gone on until the umps had gotten irritated enough to start tossing pitchers.

It was cleaner this way, even if I was going to get fined by the league. I wouldn't even fight it. I'd pay and never think about it again. Amity knew how baseball was. She knew that this happened sometimes, but I was reminded of a conversation we'd had very similar to this one when I'd been in high school, only it'd been her brother who'd gotten into the fight.

She hadn't liked it then, either.

When she was done with her cookies, we settled back into bed and I thought we were going to go to sleep. As it was, I was off schedule. We had two games tomorrow, which meant I needed to be at the field earlier than normal. Which should've meant that I went to sleep a little earlier. Sleep was an important part of what I did. I could be kind of tired for one game, but that couldn't be the norm. I wouldn't play well.

But then Amity climbed on top of me after the lights were out and there was zero chance I was going to tell her I had to go to sleep.

This was slower. She kissed me and rubbed her

pussy against my cock. It had already been hard the moment she'd climbed on. It didn't need the help.

I let her have the control she clearly wanted and when she freed my cock from my boxers and impaled herself with it, I just fucking enjoyed the ride.

It was like she thought she needed to get her fill of me in one day. As if it were the only day she'd get to have me, but I'd spend the rest of my life proving to her that I wasn't going anywhere. Even if we could possibly be apart for a lot of the days. She wouldn't travel with the team every time, which meant being apart.

I'd make up for it when I got home.

Once she'd come, I let myself go and she slumped against me. It was only thirty seconds before she lifted off and went to the bathroom. I went in after her.

Then we finally settled in to get some sleep.

The pounding on Amity's front door woke me before the sunlight coming through the window could. It was early. Too fucking early, but as least it was daylight. I would've needed to leave within the hour anyway.

Amity tiredly pushed up and swung herself out of the bed. Before leaving the room, she pulled on her pajama shirt and shorts then headed to the door. While she did that, I got myself dressed and ran my hands through my hair.

Didn't matter how much I wanted to stay—I had to go to work.

"You gave me a heart attack," her father's voice boomed.

Fuck. Not exactly the morning I'd wanted.

"It's early, Dad. I was sleeping, but I'm fine." The door shut, which meant he'd come inside.

There was no use in hiding the fact that I was here. First of all, I wanted everyone to know she was mine. Second, I had to leave, which meant going by them at the door. So I headed out there.

Mr. Kincaid's gaze hopped to me as soon as he saw the movement. If I had to guess, I'd say that both Amity and I looked like what we'd been doing last night. At the very least, he knew I'd spent the night in his daughter's bed.

Then he looked back to Amity. "This isn't what I had in mind when I said I wanted someone to stay the night with you."

I fought a smile, but Amity snickered. "Well, you weren't really clear on that."

When I got to them, I didn't bother greeting him. We were past that already.

"I have to go," I told her quietly, to which she nodded. She knew the schedule. I leaned down to get my shoes and when I stood again, I pinched her chin between my finger and thumb then leaned in to kiss her. It was a quick goodbye. Nothing more. Her father was standing right there. "I'll see you after the game. Nice to see you, Coach." He'd always be Coach to me.

She nodded, then I left her apartment.

A tiny bit of me felt like a dick leaving her there to deal with her dad alone, but I didn't have a choice and knew Amity would defuse him if he needed diffusing.

My focus now needed to be on the game.

CHAPTER 15
AMITY

"As you can see, I'm fine," I said to my dad as I went to the kitchen for a drink. That wasn't exactly how I'd wanted to wake up this morning.

In my mind, I would've slowly woken with the light while being snuggled in Silas's arms. Not yanked from bed by a concerned father pounding on my door.

"Do you want a drink?" I asked as I pulled a bottle of water from the fridge. I used refillable bottles because the disposable ones made me feel bad. This way, I wasn't adding to the environmental problem.

"I'm good." He leaned his arms on the small

island in my kitchen. Dad wasn't fifty yet, but he did have a few gray hairs creeping in at the temples. His skin was tanned from all of his time outside coaching baseball, but he always wore sunscreen, so I wouldn't worry about future problems. He was also still in good shape and today he wasn't wearing his uniform. He only did that when at games. He was probably headed to the school to watch tapes or whatever.

Most coaches taught **PE** or something else along with coaching, but given the highly sought-after program that he'd created, he only coached base-ball. Nothing more. Then he had the rest of the summer off though he started baseball camp in the fall and made and entire workout schedule for the players for the entire year. It wasn't like he only worked during baseball season.

"I wanted to check on you," he told me as if he knew I was wondering what he was doing here so early. In reality, it wasn't so early. Almost eight and thankfully, he'd knocked. Who knew how much longer Silas and I would've slept. Then he would've been late getting to the field.

"Like I said. I'm fine. It was a major accident for my car, but very minor for me." I shrugged my shoulders exaggeratedly. "Little soreness from the seatbelt. That's it. Didn't hit my head. Didn't break anything."

"What happened?"

I sighed then moved over to sit at the table. Dad came with me and took the chair on the other side. "The guy ran the red light. Smashed into the front of my car, but on the side. Pushed me into the other lane. Luckily, I didn't hit any other cars."

"Was the guy drunk?" His jaw tensed. Car accidents were a definite sore spot for him and me.

I nodded. "I saw the paramedic at the hospital after they brought him in. She said he was arrested for driving under the influence and needed to come in for a blood test." I took another drink. "I don't know that she was supposed to tell me that, but she did."

"God damn it," he muttered. "I'm going to cover you in bubble wrap to keep you safe."

I snorted. He'd said this more than once since Jayce had died. "It freaked me out, too, Dad." I swallowed hard. "And Silas. That's why he was here."

Dad worked the muscle in his jaw for several moments before replying. "I'm sure it did freak him out, as you put it. Is that the only reason he was here?"

"No." I couldn't lie to my father. In fact, I'd always been closest with him. To me, Mom had been aloof and cold my entire childhood. The way she'd just up and left after the worst thing in all of our lives had happened showed that very thing.

"He kissed you in front of me, so I assumed." He sat back heavily in his chair and sighed. I didn't hide anything from Dad and honestly, we talked about more personal things than I think most people talked to their dads about. It was just the way we were. He wasn't squeamish to know his daughter was having sex or anything else I might've told him. Did he love it? No, but he wasn't going to shut me down because it might be uncomfortable. "Please tell me he didn't try to have sex with you last night."

I bit my lips together but didn't answer. I didn't need to.

"Damn it, Amity. You were in an accident last night."

"I was, but I was also fine. The doctors found nothing wrong with me." I scooched my chair closer to him. "You know I liked Silas back when I was too young to know better. I'm not too young now, but I still don't know any better."

"You're right about that." His dark eyes met

mine. My eyes were the one feature of my mom's that I was most happy to have. They were different and they were beautiful. "He better not hurt you, Amity. You know baseball players—"

"I do. And I know the risk I'm taking, but I'm taking it." Because my brother's death had taught me that I wasn't going to miss an opportunity at something I wanted because I was scared or nervous. If I got hurt with Silas, I'd likely never recover, but that wasn't worth not taking the chance.

"All right." Dad pushed up from the table. I followed and then he took me into his arms in a big, bear hug. "I've got to get to work." His season was in full swing, too.

"I'll look at your schedule and find some games to come to," I told him. High school baseball was as entertaining to me as the Major Leagues and Dad's team was doing really well right now. If they made the playoffs, which they would, I'd be at those games too unless I had to travel for work.

"Yeah." He squeezed me a little tighter and rubbed my back before releasing me. My guess was that he'd needed that hug as much as I always did. My dad gave the best hugs and since I'd been in an accident and bad memories were coming to the surface, he would've needed to hold me at least for a moment. "Dinner, too. Sunday?"

"I can do that." I didn't work Sunday and the team wasn't traveling for another week, so I knew I could commit.

As if it pained him, he added, "It's a day game for Silas. If he wants to come, he can."

I giggled. "That is a delightful invitation, Father."

"You need to meet Diane, anyway." He headed toward the door.

I slapped his back twice and in my best "fatherly" voice said, "I hope you're behaving yourself with that woman."

Dad turned and shook his head. "I'm absolutely not."

"*Dad*!" That wasn't what I had expected him to say. "I can't believe you just said that."

He held up his hands in defense. "Hey. If you're going to tell me what happened with you and Silas last night, then I'm telling you about my love life. Fair is fair."

"Go to work," I said through a groan.

He kissed my forehead then left.

Honestly, hearing about my dad's relationship

didn't bother me. It didn't gross me out, either. If fact, I was happy for him.

Since my mother had left, my dad had probably dated and probably had sex with some of them. I didn't get the details and I didn't want to. But this woman was the first one that he wanted me to meet. That meant something.

I wanted this for him.

I needed to shower and get to work.

When I got into the office, I was surprised to find that today was a double header to make up for a rained-out game at the start of the season. The guys would get a little time between games but wouldn't go anywhere because they'd need to eat and change and power up for the next game. After seeing it on the schedule, I remembered it being there. At first I only paid attention to when the travel days were.

I was an hour into work when there was a quick knock on my open door and Camden came rushing in.

"Are you all right?" she asked.

"I'm fine. It wasn't a bad accident, but my car is totaled. My dad didn't want me taking an Uber."

She came over behind the desk to hug me then

went back to the chair across from me. "Rightfully so."

"Thanks for saying you'd come get me. I appreciate it." I rested my arms on my desk because I wasn't even going to pretend to be working while we talked.

"Yeah. My brother hijacked it, though." She rolled her eyes. "When he heard you were in an accident I thought he was going to lose it. He said he was going then hauled ass out of the house. I'm sorry if you didn't want him to come."

I snorted. "It's fine. I just needed a ride home. I called you because my dad wanted someone to spend the night in case I had a problem. It was all good."

She scowled. "Did my brother leave you alone?"

"He did not."

She searched my face as if she thought she'd discover the truth if I were lying. I wasn't lying and I guess she decided she didn't need the details and adjusted in her seat.

"It's because of my brother," I told her. "That he freaked out. I think everyone around that is still traumatized."

"I understand and I would've stayed with you."

"Thank you."

Because as I thought earlier, Camden had become my best female friend. Over all, my dad was my best friend and I didn't care how corny it was to say that. I'd had friends while I'd been away from Kalamazoo and some were people I'd keep in touch with. They were real friends, but I didn't open up to anyone very often.

"Are you going to the games?" she asked as she stood. "I am and I'm using Dad's season tickets if you want one. They're right by the dugout, so I can harass my brothers whenever one of them come up to bat."

"Oh, they'll love that. Can't wait until we play Urban's team."

She gave me a big grin. "Two weeks."

Camden's relationship with her brothers was enviable, but Urban was going to be pissed if she did mess with him while he was batting. Though it was unlikely anything she said would get through to him. The guys were masters at tuning out the crowd when they needed to focus.

"Yeah. I'll come with you," I told her because I could do that. I'd been gone over the weekend and my schedule wasn't set anyway.

"Meet you in the concourse," she said as she left the office.

I hadn't planned on going to a game today and certainly wasn't dressed for it, but I'd be fine.

That afternoon around twelve-thirty, I joined Camden in the concourse, then we headed down to her seats. The guys were doing their stretches and generally warming up. It was hard not to watch a bunch of fit men doing the things they were doing, but it was the hardest not to watch Silas.

If he was tired from last night, he wasn't showing it, but I'd bet he was going to be wiped out tonight.

When it was time for them to take the field, they all trotted back to the dugout to get their gloves. That was when Silas saw me there with his sister. My sunglasses blocked him from seeing that I was watching him, but he knew. Of course he knew.

One corner of his mouth turned up and he gave me the guy nod. It was all the recognition I was going to get because he was focused on the game. I didn't need any, though. He knew I was there and that was enough.

Our team won that game, but it was close. It seemed every time we scored, the other team did too. We only won by a single run and both sides had to do it all again at seven. It was only a little over two hours away. I wondered if any of them would catch a nap in the clubhouse.

"Want to go get food before the next game?" Camden asked as we filed out with everyone else.

"You want me to come tonight?" I asked her.

"I do. Harlowe likes baseball, but she works all the freaking time. I don't have anyone else I'd want to ask, other than her or you." She turned into the concourse and I was right by her side. "What am I going to do? Ask my dad? No, thank you."

I chuckled. I couldn't imagine watching a game with the great Conrad Briggs had gotten easier than it had been in high school. He hadn't gone to all of the games, but when he had, it had been brutal. My dad had to shut him down a few times and that had created some not-so-great feelings between them.

After all, Dad was just a high school coach. Who was he to shut down a future Hall of Famer?

"Yeah. Let's get some food."

"How about I call Harlow and have her start something for us? I could use a big cheeseburger."

"Same. I like everything on it. I just have to go grab my purse and shut things down."

We made a plan to meet back there in twenty. She'd take care of the food and hopefully, Harlowe would be able to take a break to join us.

After I got my purse and shut my office down, I decided to take the long way back. Yes. I thought maybe I could catch a minute with Silas just to touch base, but before I could get down there, he sent a text.

Are you around? I'd love to see you for a minute.

That brought a smile to my face. He wanted to see me. *Where?*

I'm by our exit. There were some fans.

Then that was where I'd head.

Fans was an understatement. I shouldn't have thought that. There were fans and the women surrounding Silas were probably fans of something. Not to be catty. They could've loved baseball. They were also fans of *his.*

One kept touching his arm as I approached, which he immediately shook off each time, but that didn't deter her at all.

The last thing I wanted to do was approach like a jealous girlfriend, but I'd be lying if I said I didn't have a rock sitting in my stomach.

He had opportunity to be with whomever he wanted. Almost no one would likely turn him down, but that was my insecurity. Not his problem to deal with.

I stopped a bit away and watched. Like he could

feel my eyes on him, he turned, then smiled when he saw me. He mumbled something to the fans then turned to come toward me.

"How long have you been here?" he asked, though he didn't lean in to kiss me and that was a good thing. We were at work, after all.

"Not long."

"Something wrong?" He raised an eyebrow. It must've been my voice that had given me away.

"No."

He furrowed his brows then gently wrapped his hand around my bicep to pull me away. Once we were off to the side where no one could see us, he leaned in closer and asked, "You sure?"

"Yeah. That whole thing just plays on some insecurities, but they're mine and I'll deal with them." I waved back at the entrance as I spoke.

"Fans?"

I cocked my head to the side, narrowed my eyes, and pursed my lips. "*Some* fans in particular."

"Ah." At least now he knew what I was talking about.

"Just reminds me of all the time I spent watching you, your brothers, my brother with other girls."

"Watching?"

I gave him a light shove. "Not watching like *that*. But you were all hoes because the baseball team could get anyone they wanted."

"Did any of the baseball team want you? Other than me?" His tone sounded like he was trying to make it seem like he was joking yet also wasn't.

"Are you kidding me? You met you guys in high school, right? No one would get near me. That lasted long after you left because there was always another Briggs brother."

Now he smiled widely. "Good." But then he brushed his fingers over my cheek and leaned in close so there could be no mistaking that he was talking to me alone. "I was only like that then because I couldn't have you. You were one of my best friends' sisters. I couldn't do that."

"Yeah, yeah. Like I said… It's something for me to deal with."

"I won't hurt you, Amity. Not now that I have you. I won't chance losing you"

"I know," I said quietly. "Want to hear about my dad's visit?"

He chuckled. "Yeah, actually."

After I filled him in quickly, he groaned. "I can't believe you told him we had sex. I mean, I don't really care because we're grown, but he doesn't need to know."

I shrugged. "I tell my dad everything." Then I glanced at the time on my phone. "I have to go meet your sister for burgers."

"You coming to the game tonight?"

"I am. Your sister wants me to."

"*I* want you to." He ran his nose over my cheek then whispered, "I want to kiss you so fucking bad right now."

But we were out in the open and that would've been bad. There was a code of conduct for the players and the staff, actually. We shouldn't even be as close as we were.

"You're just going to have to wait until later."

He swallowed hard. "I can't spend the night with you tonight."

"That's fine." Though I hadn't expected him to.

"I'm going to be beat after the next game. With the little sleep I had last night and the guarantee of losing sleep tonight if I stay with you… I have to go home."

I snickered. "I know, Silas. I didn't think you'd be there tonight. It's fine. You're kissing needs will just have to wait."

"Fuck that," he said as he moved away from me.

There were voices getting closer. "I'll see you tonight. It'll just be so I can kiss you, though. Don't try to convince me of more."

He began backing away but didn't turn.

"I think you're big enough to resist me."

He threw his hands out and let them fall. "I'm a weak man, Amity."

That wasn't true in most of his life, but maybe it was only me that made him weak.

I didn't hate the idea and couldn't wait to kiss him goodnight.

CHAPTER 16
SILAS

his week had been busier than most weeks were. Too fucking busy, if I were being honest.

With both Amity and me running around, I barely got a chance to see her. I did talk to her every day and couldn't fucking wait to see that shy smile on her face when we happened to see each other at the ballpark. But our schedule was a bear and she understood that I had to keep my routine.

The stereotype of the professional athlete going out every night, drinking to their heart's desire, was a myth. Or at least it was to me. I did know guys who did that. But if I wanted to stay at the top of my game, during the season, I had to stay on track.

Did that mean that before Amity had come

back that I hadn't fucked around? No. I sure as fuck had. But you could hook up and still be in bed in enough time to wake up rested for the next game. I didn't drink much at all during the season.

I was focused and for the first time, I began to wonder if I was *too* focused.

I loved this game. Loved that I got to play it, but loving it meant not seeing Amity and that, I fucking hated.

We headed out to Boston, but Amity didn't go on this trip. Her boss, Peggy, did. That was what we were used to. Peggy had worked for the team for years. Longer than I'd been here, but I sure as hell would've preferred Amity go with us.

This was one of the toughest series on our schedule. We always had a hard time with Boston and knew the four-day series was going to be brutal. That meant working harder. We ended up splitting the series, which was annoying.

Amity was waiting for me after the second game of a two-game series back in Kalamazoo that Saturday. She was sitting on the floor outside the clubhouse with my sister wearing jean shorts and a loose tank top along with a pair of Converses. She looked more like a college kid than a grown-ass adult, but fuck, she was hot as hell. Her long, auburn hair was pulled up in a bun. Today had been surprisingly warm in April in Michigan. It was almost May, so it happened.

When I came out, the two of them were giggling at something on my sister's phone. Until they saw me and both stood.

"That was quick," Amity said, pointing out that I'd taken a shower in minutes to get out here with her. I wanted to see her tonight, but this time, she couldn't. She had plans with my sister, which was annoying. Though I had been the one to tell her I needed to focus this week. We had a day game tomorrow and after that, she was mine. Or rather, I was hers, considering we were going to dinner at her dad's house.

"Knew you were waiting," I told her as she picked herself up from the floor.

I didn't give a fuck that my little sister was standing next to us. I cupped Amity's cheek and kissed her. Her mouth was soft and responsive. The taste of her got me hard in less time than it took for me to bring my mouth to hers. The smell of cotton candy surrounded me. That was Amity. Not anything in the tunnel. I thought it was her perfume.

She had my mouth watering.

If there was anything being on the road did, it was make me miss her and want her even more. It also forced communication. I couldn't be gone for a week or sometimes more and just not talk to her. I *needed* to talk to her. Wanted to the way I hadn't before. This week had been rough for that, but I'd still found time to call her every night.

"You know I'm standing right here, don't you?" Camden asked. When I ignored her and kept kissing my girl, she said, "Gross. I just saw tongue."

OK. That was enough. I brought the kiss to an end, even though I really didn't want to. Little sisters were a pain in the ass.

"You don't need to be here," I told her once I'd moved away from Amity, though I kept my arm around her waist and my hand on her hip.

"Yeah, I do," she countered. "I drove Amity and we have plans tonight, so…"

I shook my head then turned to Amity. "Do you really have to go out with her tonight?"

She snickered. "I do. Besides, you're the one who said you couldn't get together until tomorrow." She held her hands up in front of her. "I'm just following your lead."

At the same time that I fucking hated that Amity wasn't going to change her plans because I'd changed my mind, I loved it. She wasn't clingy. Didn't care that I wasn't always around or rather, she understood it. There was no pressure there and it made me want her even more.

"Yeah, yeah," I muttered as Jenner and Brooks joined us. Brooks was stretching his shoulder as he approached. He'd gotten hit pretty hard by a runner coming into home. His shoulder had taken the brunt of it. Catchers' bodies got beaten up regularly and it made me wonder how long he was going to stay in the game.

I hoped for a while at least, given that he was the best catcher currently in the Major Leagues.

"We need to talk to my mom," I told her quietly, knowing that everyone around us would be able to hear it anyway.

"Uh… we do?" She looked up at me with those big, gray eyes full of apprehension.

"You think it'd be better for some gossip to find her instead?"

"Gossip?"

"Amity," Jenner said while shaking his head. "You're acting purposefully thick and it's not cute."

"Watch it," I told him. No one was going to talk to her like that with me around.

"No." She set her hand on my chest. "He's

right. I am. I know we have to. I just don't want to. I like my job. And it'd be kind of nice to pretend that no one else knew. Your dad saw you kiss me so he probably already told your mom."

"He wouldn't," I assured her. "He'd hope it would go away."

"People know," Camden countered. She shrugged when Amity turned to her. "What? People do. Not a ton of people, but people."

"I just mean *widely* known," she countered, then she turned back to me, catching my gaze with those eyes I couldn't fucking ignore. "Until we know where this is going."

Brooks snorted and I could've put my fist through his teeth. This really should've been a conversation we were having alone. But we weren't and I didn't fucking care what my brother and best friend knew.

"*I* know," I told her. "I've got you now. You think I'm going to fuck that up? Think I want to lose you? Not a chance."

Her breath caught in her throat and her lips parted like she was going to say something, but words never came out.

"We'll tell her Monday. Before the charity game."

The annual charity game to benefit sports in low-income areas. Sports, not just baseball, though that was what I preferred, offered kids the opportunity to be a part of something. Create their own families. Hell, it forced those who struggled to at least have average grades. Couldn't play if your grades dropped.

Unfortunately, in a lot areas, it was also cost prohibitive. So every year, Dad had a charity game early in the season so that programs could apply for the money for the next year. Dad was an asshole in a lot of ways, but this was a good thing he did. He'd been doing it since he'd retired over ten years ago. It had started small, but as his kids had become professional athletes, along with his pull, it grew every year. Now it wasn't quite on the level of the All Star Game in July, but it was getting there.

At this point, it was an off game for most teams so that some of their better-playing guys could participate. It brought people to the stadium here in Kalamazoo and brought in the money. He gave away every single penny plus more out of his own pocket every year. The players all made big donations as well.

Plus, Amity would be at that game. All of my

brothers would be too. It was a cross between a charity game and a family one.

"Fine," she said grudgingly with her bottom lip pouted out.

"It'll be fine, Amity," Brooks assured her. "Mom likes you. Pretty sure she's wanted you with one of us since you were a kid."

My jaw tightened. Not because Brooks was wrong, but because he wasn't. Mom would be ecstatic if Amity was with any of her sons. It was the thought that ran through my head when he'd said it that pissed me off.

"Come here," I told her as I pulled her against me and cupped her cheek with my hand. When my lips touched hers, it was like the group around us faded away and it was just her and me. I was in no rush to end this particular kiss, but for some reason, this feeling deep in my gut brought me out of it. We were still kissing, but it was like her brother was standing over my shoulder reminding me that she didn't know the truth about the night he'd died.

That it had been my fault.

That if not for me, Jayce would've still been alive and probably playing this game right along with the rest of us.

Fuck.

That was a cold bucket of water all over me.

"Come on," Camden whined while yanking on Amity's arm, which forced me to bring that kiss to an end. It was like she was content to let my sister pull on her all she wanted and still wouldn't end that kiss.

"I'll see you tomorrow," I told her before letting her go.

Amity's cheeks were brushed with pink as my sister dragged her away.

Neither of the guys said a word to me as we headed out to our cars.

I'd asked for the time to focus. I'd been the one to say I couldn't see Amity this week because I'd thought that was what I needed.

But fuck, was my apartment quiet that night. She hadn't even been here yet and I missed her being there.

I was fucking gone.

That night also gave me too much time alone with my thoughts. With Jayce popping up while I'd been kissing his sister, he was all I could think of. All I could see was him slumped over the steering wheel on a deflated airbag.

Fuck.

I was going to have to tell her, wasn't I?

That it was my fault her brother was dead.

That he'd have been alive if I weren't such a fucking asshole.

There was no reason for her to know, I decided. No reason to tell her. It wouldn't change anything. And her dad knew the truth but didn't say anything which meant he must've agreed with me. I knew he hadn't told her because if he had… Amity wouldn't be in the same state as me.

Instead of dwelling, I had a beer then went to bed early. We had a day game tomorrow and needed to be at the field earlier than for night games.

Still, I waited to see if Amity sent a text when she got home. I had already sent one to my sister telling her to let me know that Amity got dropped off. First, I didn't want Amity to think she had to check in with me or that she had to answer to me or any of that bullshit. Second, I just wanted to know she was safely at home locked away in her apartment.

It was only around eleven when it came through.

You told your sister to tell you when she dropped me off?

Yup. I had nothing to hide. Amity was all I'd ever wanted and now that I had her, I needed to know she was safe. *Fuck*. I'd always wanted to know she was all right, but it wasn't until now that I'd had the right to ask.

She's not texting you. This is your notice that I'm home. My door is locked and I'm getting ready for bed.

I groaned because it was all I could do not to rush over there just to sleep with her tonight. *Good.*

Why didn't you just tell me to text you when I got home?

Didn't want you to think I'm a stalker.

Those damn dots popped up then disappeared twice, which made me think that Amity was trying to say something in just the right way. Finally, her text came through. *I wouldn't think you're a stalker. I'd just think that you cared.*

I do care.

Good. I care too. I shouldn't say this over text, but I love you and love the fact that you want to check up on me.

My fucking stomach dropped like I'd been taken down the first hill on an incredibly high roller-coaster. I couldn't text her back. This needed at least a phone call. Instead of calling, I chose Facetime.

Amity's face filled the screen. She had her auburn hair down over her bare shoulders and she'd washed off any makeup she'd had on earlier. She'd also changed into a tank top and I had to assume sleep shorts because I couldn't see that much of her.

"I thought that might bring a phone call," she said with a playful tilt to her voice. "Too much?"

"Not too much." I cleared my throat to try to clear away the emotions. Not from me. Just from my voice. "But I thought it deserved at least a phone call." We stared at each other for thirty seconds. The corners of her mouth turned up slightly. "Are you drunk?"

Her face exploded with laughter. The sound of a fucking angel. "Not unless you can get drunk on lemonade. I'm not looking to repeat my amazing performance that night at Kegs."

The night I'd held her hair back while she'd emptied her stomach. "Good plan." After readjusting myself on my bed so that I was sitting up slightly, I asked, "So you're not drunk, but you love me?"

She rolled those beautiful eyes. "Don't tell me you're surprised. Maybe surprised that I said it, but yes, Silas. I love you. You had to have known that."

The thing was, I hadn't. Had I known she'd had a crush on me when we were teenagers? Yeah. She hadn't exactly hidden it, so it had been easy to guess. Had I known that she loved me now? Not until she'd said it.

"I didn't," I told her. "I do now." She tucked her hair behind her ear shyly. "I'm coming over."

Her eyes widened. "No. You can't. It's too late for you. You have a game tomorrow."

I pushed out of my bed. "Do you think I give a shit about the game tomorrow?"

"Yes," she said seriously and she was right. I did care about the game tomorrow. It was my job and I fucking loved it.

Fuck. She was right. If I went over there right now, I wouldn't sleep at all. Neither would she, if I had anything to say about it. "Fine." I finally gave in. "I won't come over there tonight." I dropped back onto my bed. "But know that you telling me not to is the only thing keeping me from you, Amity."

She tilted her head and bit into her bottom lip. "It's for your own good."

She wasn't wrong, but fuck, I hated it right that second.

"I better let you get your beauty sleep," she told me and while I wanted to argue, I didn't.

I told her *goodnight* and waited for her to hang up.

I didn't say it back. I could've, but I didn't and there was a reason for that. The first time I told Amity that I loved her, I wanted her in front of me. Wanted my damn hands on her.

Her words had made me hard and it was going to be a long fucking night until I could see her tomorrow.

CHAPTER 17
SILAS

Unfortunately, I didn't see Amity that morning at the park or at the game. It was Sunday. She didn't work and wasn't required to be at every single one of my games, even if I wanted her to be. I was meeting her at her dad's house tonight for dinner but had no idea what she was doing today.

I played the way I was supposed to and took first place in the bet back from Jenner. It was the last day to do it too.

We ran our bets until the charity game every year. It would've been too much to go the whole season—and I won.

That victory felt less special than it usually did because all I wanted was to get to Amity.

The game ended around four and with everything I had to do after, I'd get to her dad's just before six, when the dinner was.

"You're not going to razz me?" Jenner asked when he sat in the chair beside me. Our lockers were next to each other's in the clubhouse. My brother's was on the other side.

"About?" My mind was not on the game we'd just played or anything else Jenner might've been thinking.

"The bet, of course." He tossed his deodorant back into the locker. We'd all just showered the sweat and dirt off.

"Nah. I think the sting of defeat is enough." Plus, I wanted to get the fuck out of there.

"It's Amity," Brooks told him. "He's got a date with her tonight."

"Dinner at her dad's," I corrected him. It wasn't really a date the way he meant it. Not with her dad there, anyway.

"Oh, Daddy needs to chaperone?" Jenner asked. I just raised my middle finger his way and left it at that.

Luckily, I was able to get ready in the clubhouse and head right to her dad's. Our manager had talked longer than I would've liked and I'd been antsy, bouncing my knee, the entire time. It'd been a long week without her.

We might not have been doing this long, but I'd already grown accustomed to being with her. Not to mention, she'd told me she loved me last night and I wanted the chance to say it back, even if the idea tightened my stomach. I'd never been in love with anyone else because I'd always loved Amity and couldn't have her. Shouldn't have her now. If she knew the truth… Well, I didn't want to think about what she'd do.

Everyone had told me to get over it and I tried. But how do you get over being the reason one of your best friends was dead?

Finally, I was knocking on her dad's door only a few minutes before six. I'd wanted to be here a little earlier, but this had been the best I could do.

Amity pulled the door open with just a hint of a grin on her face.

Her auburn hair was in waves down her back. Her gray eyes sparkled as she wore a sundress that came to just above her knees and sandals.

"You're here," she said as that smile played on her lips.

"Of course I am." I reached out to wrap my hand around her wrist and pulled her out the door until she slammed into my body. The smell of cotton candy engulfed me and had my mouth watering. I'd never be able to smell cotton candy again without thinking about this woman.

Then I pushed my fingers into her hair so that I was cupping her cheek. I couldn't wait another second. I pushed my mouth to hers in what I could only call an aggressive kiss. This was my first time having my hands on her since she'd told me she loved me last night and I wasn't going to waste it.

Sure, I hadn't said it back yet, but this was showing. And I'd always been told showing was better than telling.

Her lips were soft, her skin like velvet when I brought my other hand to the other side of her face so that I could hold her right where I needed her. I traced my tongue over her lips, which made her part them, as I'd intended. I pushed my tongue into her mouth, savoring the taste of her. It wasn't mint or chocolate. It was Amity.

So fucking sweet in every way.

"Are you two coming in here or do I need to get the hose out?" Her father's voice came from the open door.

I brought that kiss to an end much quicker than

I'd originally intended, but Mr. Kincaid wasn't at the door any longer.

With my arm around her shoulders, I led her back to the door. "He wouldn't really get the hose out, would he?"

She shrugged. "He did on Martin Elrod in tenth grade."

I groaned. For two reasons. One, I didn't want to get sprayed with a hose. Two, I didn't want to think about Martin Elrod anywhere near Amity, even in tenth grade.

"I think he's in prison now," I told her about good old Martin.

She laughed loudly. "No, he's not. He's a teacher in Florida."

"I'm glad he's in Florida."

Mostly, I was joking. I wasn't worried about Martin Elrod in the slightest. No matter what he'd done with Amity in tenth grade to get the hose turned on him.

"Yes, because my tenth-grade, short-term boyfriend is a threat now." She stopped before we got to the dining room and turned to look up at me. "Do I need to worry about any of the multitude of—"

I put my hand over her mouth to stop her from

going any further. "I'm fucking with you, baby. Let's not go there."

She smiled around my hand, so I removed it, then she led me into the dining room.

Sitting at the table was a woman in her mid-forties, I'd say. She had dark-blonde hair and a friendly smile. This was obviously Kincaid's new girlfriend. If he was introducing the woman to Amity, it had to be serious. I didn't think Amity had met anyone else he'd seen over the years.

After introductions were made, I was about to take a seat next to Amity, but Mr. Kincaid clapped me on the shoulder.

"Why don't you come out to the grill with me? I have to take the steaks off," he told me and I knew that this wasn't about the steaks.

Having this man coach me through high school, which had helped put me on the track to college and professional baseball, I'd learned to read him well enough. The years since he'd coached me hadn't changed that. I'd dated, though I hadn't met any woman's parents before this, but still, I knew this was the dad talk that I'd heard my own dad have with a couple of Camden's dates. Those hadn't been boyfriends. They'd been dates.

"Be right back," I whispered into Amity's ear.

She gave me a reassuring smile as I followed him out of the room.

"You need my help to take steaks off the grill?" I asked once we were on the back deck.

"Nope," he said. As I'd expected. "What're you doing with her?"

He didn't need to tell me whom or what he was talking about. But before I could answer him, he continued.

"Amity told me what happened the night of her accident." He shook his head. "She'd been in an accident, Silas. You should've only been there to make sure she was all right."

"I was," I told him, then I scratched the back of my head. How in the hell was I supposed to tell this man that it was his daughter who'd initiated the sex we'd had? She was the one to insist she'd been fine.

I couldn't. Not if I wanted to keep my balls attached because I was certain either he would rip them off or Amity would.

He made a noise I couldn't divine the meaning of. "Leave it to my daughter."

Fuck. That meant he knew what I was saying. That it was Amity who'd been so insistent. I did not want to be standing here talking to my old baseball coach about sex with his daughter. At twenty-five, it'd been a long time since I'd had to do this at all and before, it had been my own parents giving me the warnings.

They hadn't wanted me to cause any scandal. All of us had gotten severe lectures on consent as if any of us would've done anything without the person's consent. Fuck that.

"Have you told her?" he asked and he didn't need to explain what he was talking about.

Jayce.

"No," I told him. "She'll hate me."

He shrugged. "I think you underestimate her." He flipped the steaks onto the platter and turned the grill off before taking a scrub brush to the racks. "I told you that then."

He had. I'd told him I didn't want Amity to know and he hadn't liked the idea of lying to her, even if it was a lie by omission. But he'd done it. For me. I'd been so afraid that night that I was about to lose everything after losing one of my best friends that I didn't know I'd been thinking right.

"I know you did." I wrapped my arms over my chest. "I just…"

"I understand, son." He turned to me with hard, brown eyes. It was hard for me to remember what her mother looked like because it'd been years and I'd barely seen her before that. She didn't come to Jayce's games and if she had, I'd only noticed Amity. "I understand why you didn't want to tell her then, but if you're doing this thing with my daughter, she should know. She's going to find out eventually. Hell, I'm shocked she hasn't already, but she will. Not from me. But it's going to hurt more not coming from you."

"I can't tell her." It was honest. I couldn't chance the way I knew she'd look at me.

Kincaid nodded. "That's your decision. My daughter might tell me everything"—he took a step closer—"and she does tell me *everything*, whether I want to know or not." *Fuck.* I'd known they were close, but *fuck*. This had me feeling like a fifteen-year-old kid again. "But I won't get in the middle of her relationships. She has to navigate that on her own." He paused, then added, "With my support, of course."

Meaning, if I fucked this up or hurt his daughter, she wasn't the only one I'd have to deal with. Mr. Kincaid wouldn't try to beat my ass. His disappointment would've been enough. More so than my own father's.

"And this better be more," he said as he took the tray and headed back to the house. "It better be more than some random fling, like I know you've been having with other women for years."

"It is," I assured him. And I'd assure her too.

Dinner was nice and relaxed. Sort of how dinners at home were when Dad had been on the road. He always brought a tenseness to the air that none of us had ever wanted and wanted even less now that we were grown. We didn't need him riding our asses the way he still did like we were twelve years old.

No matter how nice it was to dine like a family, though, I couldn't wait to get Amity alone.

She and I left at the same time and once we were through the front door and it was closed behind us, I asked, "Are we going to your apartment?"

"That's good with me." Though she still hadn't been to my apartment.

I hadn't bought a house because in baseball, a trade could come at any time. Though I didn't think it'd happen now that I was the Knights, there was always a shred of home. Buying never seemed worth dealing with selling if I was traded. Though it was probably time to face the fact that I was on this team for the foreseeable future. At least until my contract was up. I could always choose to reject another Knights deal but that was years off. Besides, now… I wanted somewhere for Amity if she moved in with me someday.

"Ride with me?" I asked her.

"I have my car." She pointed to the blue Jeep in the driveway. She hadn't let me go out to buy her a car after her accident but insurance didn't take long and she got this one.

"Can you leave it here? I'll bring you back to get it tomorrow."

She furrowed her brows like she wasn't understanding but then shrugged. "I can have my dad and Diane drop it at my apartment on the way to the game."

The corner of my mouth hitched up.

I just wanted her with me. There was no other reason she couldn't have driven her own car back to her own apartment. But I wanted the smell of cotton candy in my car. To linger long after she was gone. *Fuck.* I might have to get her to spray it in my car to ensure just that.

Fuck. I was a pussy at this point and Jenner would've harassed me to no end if he'd known.

Amity slid into the passenger side of the car while I climbed behind the wheel. She drove a blue Jeep. I drove a black Audi A4. I absolutely could've bought a more expensive car, but I didn't need to.

Once I'd gotten us on the road and she'd texted her dad asking him to bring her car to her apartment before the game tomorrow, I took her hand in mine.

"He has a key?"

"Yeah," she told me. "I locked my keys in the car one time when I first moved back and he insisted. So when I got this car the other day, I gave him the second key."

I laughed because I could see Kincaid telling her he had to have a spare. It made sense, though.

The patter of rain began to hit my car. It was good to get this out of the way tonight because rain out on the charity game would suck.

"Do you really tell your dad everything?" I asked her.

"Yeah. He's basically my best friend. We talk about everything. Nothing is off limits." Then she shuddered. "Though the morning after the accident, he told me he wasn't being on his best behavior with Diane. That was kind of gross."

I chuckled. "Why did he tell you that?"

"Because I told him that you weren't only there to make sure I was OK."

I groaned. "That *was* the reason I was there."

"Yeah, but we had sex."

"You're very convincing."

She gave me a great smile as if being convincing had been her plan the whole time.

"I love the rain," Amity said, then she sighed the way someone would when they were leaning back into the most comfortable chairs. For her, the rain was the most comfortable chair. She'd loved it when we'd been kids and apparently, that hadn't changed. "I love the sound of it hitting the car."

I flipped the wipers on as the rain picked up. "You can hear it in your apartment, right? Like when you're trying to go to sleep?"

"Yeah." She glanced at me as she bit into her bottom lip and rubbed her legs together slightly, the motion bringing my cock to life. "It's not the same, though. This is like the patter of a drum… um… like a buildup."

"Buildup?"

She nervously bit that lip again and nodded. The rain was turning my girl on. Or maybe it was the combination of the rain and us finally being together. I'd like to think that I played a role.

This, I could work with.

I took the next turn, which I wouldn't have

done to get to her apartment. Then I pulled into the dirt driveway of a small park that would be abandoned at this time even without the rain. It wasn't fully dark yet, but we were on our way. We'd been at her dad's house for a couple of hours.

"What're we doing here?" she asked as I parked and she glanced around to see that no one was there.

"Doesn't sound like you can wait until we get to your apartment."

At first, she scrunched her eyebrows down like she didn't understand what I was talking about. So I said, "Take off your panties and come here."

That was when realization hit her and those furrowed brows were gone to be replaced by exactly what she'd been feeling. Desire.

She quickly pushed her panties down her legs and just knowing that there wouldn't be anything between us had my cock turning to granite. While she did that, I hit the locks on the door and pushed my seat all the way back to give us that extra room. It didn't have far to go, but every inch counted.

Then she scurried over until she was straddling my legs. I hadn't undone my pants yet because I hadn't been sure how far she'd let this go.

I grabbed her hips and pushed her down onto

me. The light sound of the radio played in the background. No idea what song or even what channel I had it on. Whatever it was worked to create a feeling in the car. I'd also left it running so the air conditioning would continue to blow. It was raining, but it was hot and humid.

There was no brushing of the lips here. When her lips touched mine, I devoured her. Even more than on the porch at her dad's house.

Here we had privacy.

Amity rested her hands on my shoulders as mine slid up her thighs. Given the way she was sitting, her knees were spread far enough apart for me to get my fingers between them.

As we worked our mouths together, I grazed my fingers between her legs, causing her breath to catch. She was already wet for me. My only regret in this moment was that given where we were and the amount of space we had, I wasn't going to get to taste her.

I'd still make her feel good, though.

When I pushed two fingers into her, Amity dropped her head back and muttered, "Ohmygod," as if she didn't think I could hear her.

I fucking loved it.

With the hand whose fingers weren't currently

in Amity's pussy, I pushed into her hair and tight-ened my fist. I wasn't pulling her hair, exactly, but it was firm. She leaned into it.

I had no idea if she knew she was doing it, but her hips were moving in time with me. She was fucking herself on my fingers as much as I was fucking her with them.

When I brushed across her clit with my thumb, one of her hands shot out and braced herself on the window.

There wasn't a thing in this world that could've gotten me to stop right then.

I continued working her over as I released her hair to pull the strap of her dress and bra down, freeing one of her tits. Her nipple was hard and tight when I took it in my mouth, causing her groan.

It wasn't but thirty seconds later that she came on my hand and her hips slowed to a stop. Her breathing was erratic and her skin flushed with the most beautiful pink hue I'd ever seen. I wanted inside her so fucking badly but would wait until her apartment if she wanted to.

Slowly, I pulled my fingers out of her as she watched me.

Apparently, I wasn't moving fast enough

because she said, "Are you going to get your pants off?"

Didn't have to ask me twice. I used both hands to push them down with her on top of me. I wasn't sure how we had enough room, but we made it work.

I'd barely finished when Amity wrapped her fist around my cock then settled herself all the way down me.

"Fuck," I groaned. She felt so fucking good. She didn't hesitate at all.

I grabbed her hips again but didn't need to.

Amity was already riding me like she'd been born to do it. She braced her hands against the roof of the car, though I pulled the other side of her dress and bra down so that I could cup her tits.

She felt amazing sliding against me and given our location, I wasn't even going to try to hold out. This might have been a quick one, but fuck if it wasn't just as good.

After I released into her, she slowed, placed her hands on my cheeks, and kissed me. This time, it was slower, less urgent, and I was pretty sure she'd come a second time.

"Want to take me home now?" she asked as she tiredly laid her head against my shoulder.

"Absolutely."

I waited until she'd put herself back together and settled into the seat with her seatbelt on before driving us out of that park.

I'd never been more grateful for knowing this park was here and what she didn't know was that I wasn't done with her.

Not by a long shot.

CHAPTER 18
AMITY

My bedroom was like a cocoon where only Silas and I existed.

At least for those few hours we were alone and no one bothered us. We were able to lie in each other's arms and talk quietly, as if someone else would hear us, even though there wasn't another soul in the apartment. I assumed it would be the same at his, but I hadn't been there yet.

The alarm went off too early the next morning, though I'd made sure to quiet down at a decent hour so that Silas could get some sleep. Today's game was a charity one, but he still needed his rest. My dad always said that a tired player became an injured player.

I didn't want that for him and certainly not because of me.

But when my alarm went off, the bed next to me was empty and the shower was going in the bathroom. Silas must've set his earlier than mine and I hadn't even heard it.

I pushed the blanket back and quickly made my way to the bathroom. After tapping on it lightly, I cracked the door open and said, "Good morning."

"Come in," he called out, so I did as he demanded.

My bathroom had been recently updated and the shower was one of the main reasons I'd decided on this place. It had glass doors and no step up. Plus, it was roomy enough for more people than I'd ever consider having in there.

Which meant I could see every inch of Silas and every move he made.

He was intoxicating, but I was an addict who stood no chance where he was concerned.

"What time did you get up?" I asked.

He chuckled. "Not long ago. Figured I'd get the day started. You looked so peaceful sleeping that I didn't want to wake you." The shower cut out, then he opened the door and grabbed the towel hanging just outside of it. "And I thought you might need the rest after last night."

The cocky grin he was trying to keep a handle on wasn't cocky to me. It was sexy as hell.

But he was right. I had needed sleep after last night. Him stopping at that park had surprised me, especially since he was very recognizable in Kalamazoo. Anyone would've known it was him.

"What time do you need to be at the park?" I asked instead of letting my memories slide into a place that would make it inappropriate to be around both of our families in a little while.

"Not for a while, but we're going early." He ran that towel down the hard plane of his chest and abdomen then over his balls before wrapping it around his waist.

"We are?" That was news to me.

"Gotta talk to my mom."

Oh. Right. I took a deep breath because this wasn't something I was looking forward to.

Most of the time when I dated a guy, I never met their parents, let alone had to tell one of them we were together because it could impact my job otherwise. She might've already known if his dad told her he saw him kiss me but we still had to do it officially.

"Right." The tone I hadn't meant to be there was.

Silas chuckled then rested his hands on my shoulders. "It'll be fine, Amity." Then he shrugged. "Though I don't give a fuck if it's not fine. I've got you now. I'm not changing that because of anything anyone says."

I scowled and muttered, "You've got me. Pfh."

He laughed again. This man was in far too good of a mood for it being morning. Maybe I just wasn't a morning person. "You've got me," he said. "So I have to assume I've got you."

Well, yeah. When you put it like that.

"Why don't you hop in the shower," he said, then he gave my ass a light slap. "I'll make some breakfast. My shower was quick. Should still be plenty of hot water."

That sounded like a good idea.

Twenty minutes later, I came out of my bedroom having showered, put on distressed jean shorts that were short, but not too short, and a T-shirt that I knew Silas would love. I'd stopped at one of the merch stands the other day. Then I pulled my hair up into a bun because while it was only May, it was supposed to be a hot day. With only the smallest amount of makeup, I was able to get ready pretty quickly.

Silas turned from the stove as I got close. It smelled like he'd made eggs and bacon, and I saw the toast already on the table.

"What're you wearing?" A smile played on his lips. He knew exactly what I was wearing.

"It's my favorite baseball team." I'd gotten a Kalamazoo Knight T-shirt that had their emblem over my left breast. The shirt was orange and the emblem white.

"I hear it's a good team." He ran his tongue over his bottom lip. "Turn around."

I snorted. These shirts had a player's name and number on the back. I knew that would be what he wanted to see.

Slowly, I turned so my back was facing him.

"Fuck, yes," he said when he saw Briggs and his number on the back. Not to be confused with his brother, though; I'd thought about buying his brother's shirt to mess with him. "You picked the right Briggs."

Yeah. Yeah.

Silas brought the two plates over to the table, where we could eat quickly. If he wanted to get to the field early, we'd have to get moving. It was a charity game and started at eleven.

"What is it with you guys?" I asked after taking a bite of scrambled egg. "Why do you like seeing your name on people? I mean, I assume it's different that *I'm* wearing your number rather than a random woman. Or I hope it is."

He reached out and ran his thumb across my cheek. "It's very different."

"So what is it, then? An ownership thing?"

"No." He finished chewing then took a quick drink of his milk. "It's not ownership." Then he paused, like he was thinking it over. "Or not owner-ship, exactly." He stopped and looked me in the eye. "I don't think I own you, but it's like… I want everyone to know you're mine. That you're with me."

"They won't know that from this shirt," I pointed out as he went back to eating. "Lots of women wear your number."

"But *I* know." And it was as simple as that, I guess. "No people won't *know* you're mine but I can pretend that they do." He scratched the back of his head. "It's akin to middle school hickey I guess."

That had me laughing loudly.

Once we were finished, I quickly loaded the

dishes into the dishwasher, grabbed my purse, and put on my Chucks for us to head to the ballpark.

For some reason, I was nervous, but I tried like hell to not show it.

Almost immediately after we arrived, my dad sent a text saying that my car was now at my apartment. We'd just missed them.

"Let's find my mom." Silas took my hand, which was a first at the ballpark, and led me up the tunnel to where he thought his mom would be. It was only a minute before we found her with some guys in suits around her.

Once she'd seen us, she ended whatever conversation she was having with them and shooed them away. Today wasn't supposed to be about work. It was about the charity. Which was one of the only selfless things I'd ever see Mr. Briggs do in the time that I'd known them.

"Hey, honey." She reached up to give Silas a quick hug. Her smile at me was genuine. Then her gaze slid down to where he was holding my hands. "Have something to tell me?"

"Yeah." Silas scratched the back of his head. "We're together. Thought you should know because Amity works here and rumors and all of that bullshit."

Mom chuckled. "I don't listen to rumors. Had to learn to ignore them a long time ago." I thought that was because she'd dated a baseball player and while Mr. Briggs hadn't played for Kalamazoo, I'd bet there had been rumors surrounding it.

Mrs. Briggs reached out to the hand that Silas wasn't holding and squeezed. "I'm very happy to hear this. At least I won't have to worry about one of my sons."

It took everything I had to not let out a donkey laugh. If she was talking romantically, she probably needed to worry about *all* of her sons, though she might've thought that Silas was mine to deal with now.

"I don't know about that, Mom." Silas squeezed my hand as his mother released the other one. "Amity's a bad influence on me."

"Uh, am not," I countered.

"Please." He only glanced at me then looked back at his mother. "If you knew what she talked me into when we left her dad's house last night, you'd be shocked."

My cheeks immediately burned.

"Rob a bank, did you?" Mrs. Briggs countered, probably knowing that wasn't what Silas was referring to but willing to pretend to save me some embarrassment. "Should I call the lawyers?"

"Nah, we weren't caught."

I slapped a hand over my face then dragged it down. "I'm really rethinking this whole thing."

Mrs. Briggs chuckled. "Don't do that. I've waited long enough for one of my sons to settle down a little. And don't worry. Raising four boys… I'm not shocked by anything anymore."

"Not until Brooks finds a woman, right?"

That sounded like an inside joke to me.

"I have faith," she told him, then she turned her attention back to me. "Amity, I'm very happy that Silas has finally taken his head out of his ass. Welcome to the family."

"I wouldn't jump right to that, Mrs. Briggs," I told her.

"AnnMarie," she said. "Call me 'AnnMarie.'"

I wondered if that meant I should call his dad 'Conrad.' Probably not. Mr. Briggs would probably have his actual daughters-in-law call him 'Mr. Briggs' after being married to one of his sons for fifty years.

"I'm still mulling," I told her regarding Silas.

"Thank fuck." Another voice came from behind us. I turned and found Brooks. "You finally got out of your own way and now I don't have to be the one to bring Amity into the family."

I snickered. It had been said that their mother had liked me when we were younger and thought I'd be perfect for one of her boys. Camden said she'd thought I'd be perfect for Silas, even though Cobb had been in my class. I thought this meant that she actually had wanted me with Silas all along.

"Fuck off," Silas countered. "I'm going to go get ready," he told his mom, then the three of us were headed back down the tunnel to the clubhouse.

"I was going to buy one of your T-shirts to wear today," I told Brooks. "Just to mess with him."

Brooks's loud laugh echoed down the tunnel. "You should have. That would've been great."

Brooks and I had always gotten along, but there had never been any sparks between us.

"Ha ha. You're both mean." Silas pulled me to a stop at the door of the clubhouse. I couldn't go in there before a game and wouldn't have wanted to. "I've got to go get ready."

"Yup. Have a good game," I told the both of them before pushing to my toes to quickly kiss Silas.

Once he'd disappeared through that door, I headed out to the seats, where I knew Camden would be. There was a big block of seats that had been bought by Mr. Briggs and doled out by all the members of the family. My dad had taken a ticket for Diane, so she'd be sitting with us as well.

No one cared what seat they sat in at this game, I was told. As long as we were in the blocked section, which was the one around the home team's dugout, we were good.

Camden waved as soon as she saw me. I hurried down to her and saw that she'd grabbed us seats right next to the dugout. There were only three in that row, which was perfect for her, Diane, and me. I'd asked her to save a seat for Diane as well. This was her first time coming to this game and I hadn't been in years. Since before any of the Briggs boys had played.

Now all four of them were here.

Brooks and Silas were on the same team because they were usually on the same team. Urban and Cobb were on the other. Those two didn't get to play with any of their brothers often. Though if their parents had any say in it, both boys would join Silas and Brooks on the Knights eventually.

Their dad wasn't shy about saying that was his dream.

"You're here." Camden reached out to hug me, which I returned.

"Hey, Diane," I said as I took my seat between them once Camden let me go.

"Did your dad text you about your car?" she asked.

My cheeks threatened to burn. "He did. Thanks for dropping that off this morning."

"Why'd they have to drop off your car?" Camden asked, but my eyes widened and I shook my head just enough for her to see it. Her face scrunched up, like she'd just smelled something awful. "Never mind. I don't want to know."

I couldn't look over at Diane. She'd laughed quickly and quietly, which made me think she knew exactly why Camden didn't want to know.

Both teams were doing their stretches. It wasn't like the regular games where the guys kind of stayed apart pre-game. This was for fun and for charity. It'd grown big enough that the league always had charity game day off. Which was why it was on a Monday. No way would they have players for a weekend game.

The four Briggs boys were clearly harassing each other as they stretched. They were too far away from us for us to hear what they were saying, but they were laughing and Silas gave Urban a shove.

Dad was managing the team Silas and Brooks were on. He was one of, if not *the*, best high school coaches in the country. Clearly, these guys played Major League and there was more than one coach, but he was the head coach.

"My brothers are so gross," Camden said, bringing me out of my own head. Then she looked over at me. "I mean, I'm glad you don't think Silas is because I like having you around. It's selfish, but whatever."

I snickered. "They aren't gross."

Diane leaned forward to look at her. "They aren't gross."

Camden and I both swung our heads around with wide eyes.

"I'd bet a lot of women in this country would agree with me," she added.

"No. They are."

"Are you… crushing on the Briggs boys?" I asked Diane while trying to keep my smile at bay.

"Obviously not. They could mostly be my kids, but they're good-looking men. I wouldn't classify them as *gross*."

Camden rolled her eyes. "That's because you didn't grow up with them."

We left it at that because it was time to start the game.

This was fun, but all the guys were so competitive that it was like having a real game, only they messed around a bit more.

I got to watch Silas enjoy the profession he'd chosen. Most of the time, he looked so serious that I wasn't sure he loved the game as much as he said he did.

But watching him here today showed that he loved it. They all did. If their dad left them alone and took off that pressure, they'd love it even more.

CHAPTER 19
AMITY

In the end, the team Urban and Cobb played for won. Either way, it was for charity and after the game, Mr. Briggs announced how much they'd raised.

It was a high enough dollar amount that I swallowed hard. It wasn't what Silas made in a year, but it was a hell of a lot more than I did.

"You're coming to the house, right?" Camden asked as we stood up to leave.

"I… don't know."

She furrowed her brows. "Even your dad is coming. Why wouldn't you?"

"Yeah." Diane nudged my shoulder and I was suddenly grateful that my father had chosen her as the first woman in his life for me to meet. She was nice and wasn't trying to be my mom. I didn't know her too well yet, but so far, we were getting along fantastically.

"Because I don't know what you're talking about." I shifted my weight from one foot to the other as a swift breeze ran over my skin. It'd been a hot day and that little bit of relief was welcomed.

"Wait." Camden grabbed my arm. "Silas didn't tell you?"

"Tell me what?"

She sighed and shook her head. "*Silas!*" she called out. I turned to see him take the steps in the dugout quickly and come to where we were standing. Now he was still on the field and we were two rows up and there was the barrier between us, but he still almost stood taller than me.

"What?" he asked. He would've recognized that it was his sister calling him.

"Why did you not invite Amity to the house? Her dad's coming, for crying out loud."

He cocked his head to the side. "I did." Then he looked at me. "I told you about it."

"Uh… you didn't."

"I did."

I sighed. "I'm not going to argue it with you,

but I have no idea why my dad's going to your house right now, so I'm thinking that you didn't."

"Fuck." He scratched the back of his head, now looking like a kid who'd gotten caught doing something he wasn't supposed to do. "Sorry. I meant to. Actually, I thought I did last night after we left your dad's house."

My eyes widened and my cheeks heated. "Uh, you definitely didn't tell me after my dad's house."

A slow, satisfied grin began to appear and I bit my lips together. Surely, he wasn't going to say anything incriminating with his sister and Diane standing right there. "That's right. There wasn't really a chance. With the rain."

My jaw tightened, but I wasn't going to respond. "So do you want me to go to your parents' house?"

"Fuck, yes," he told me. "If you're not coming, there's no reason for me to be there."

"Uh…" Camden raised her hand. "I'm there."

He snorted and shook his head but didn't respond to her, making Camden to groan.

"Whatever." She slipped her arm through mine. "I'm taking Amity with me and we'll meet you there."

He opened his mouth to protest, but she was

already pulling me away. I just shrugged. I supposed I was meeting him there.

"Now I kind of *do* want to know what you two did when you left the house," Diane said quietly from behind me, causing both Camden and me to devolve into fits of laughter.

That wasn't something I was going to tell either of them, but they could've guessed.

We walked Diane to where she could meet my dad and we waited with her until he came out. He was going home to shower off before heading to the Briggs' house. Once they were on their way, Camden and I went on ours.

First, we stopped back at my apartment so that I could pack a tote bag with my bathing suit and a change of clothes. If it cooled off once the sun set, I might want something other than these shorts. I was a *be prepared* kind of girl, even if Camden insisted that I could borrow something from her.

Then we headed to her parents' house.

When we got there, the grill was already going, but of course it wasn't Mr. Briggs at the helm like it would've been my dad at his house. They had someone grilling. A cook or personal chef. I wasn't sure, but they rarely cooked themselves.

"Who's all supposed to be here?" I asked Camden when we came through the door.

"Just the family. Your dad, you, the other coaches from the game, and probably their wives or girlfriends. It's low key."

"You're here," her mother exclaimed as she came into the entryway. Their house was large, but not one of those overblown mansions that you saw professional athletes buy. It was a mini-mansion, maybe, and where the kids had grown up.

"We're here," Camden said. "It's hot outside and you have a pool."

Her mother chuckled as if Camden didn't still live here at home. She was in college and lived on campus the first two years, even though it had been in the same city. Then she'd grown tired of dorm life, she'd said, and moved back home.

The place was big enough and her parents busy enough that it probably felt like she lived alone most of the time. For tonight, it was likely that Urban and Cobb were staying here, too. Though I assumed they'd be on their way in the morning for wherever their next game was.

"Well, you're both free to change and hop in. Though the food should be done soon." She glanced toward the door. "Hopefully, the boys will be here by then."

Camden grabbed my arm to pull me farther into the house. "If not, it just means more for us."

"As if the three of us could eat all of that."

Then we were headed up the stairs. I thought she'd direct me toward the bathroom. I hadn't been up here before. Not even when we'd been kids. Anytime I'd been to this house, I'd been downstairs.

"You can change in Silas's old room. Mom still keeps the boys' rooms up in case any of them needed to stay here." She stopped in front of the second door. "Like Urban and Cobb will just be in their own rooms tonight, but neither Silas nor Brooks have stayed here in forever." She shrugged. "They have places in town."

Yeah. That made sense.

"Thanks." Then she was gone into what I assumed was her room.

I pushed the door open slowly. Did I want to see where Silas had spent all of his time as a teenager and in the summers during college? Kind of, but I wasn't so sure.

Luckily for me, it looked like a room. Just a basic room. In the years since he'd moved out, I assumed that AnnMarie had probably had it painted.

But his high school trophies still lined a shelf on one wall. I took a couple of minutes to look at them then got an idea.

I went over to his bed, with no idea whether this was actually his bed or if it'd been replaced since he'd last stayed here, and flung myself down on top of it. Then I snapped a picture on my phone, making sure the trophies were in the background, and sent it to Silas with the text, *Guess where I am?*

It was only a few seconds before I got a video call.

"That didn't take long," I answered.

"You're in my room." His background moved in a blur which meant he was. "What're you doing in my room? Please say something dirty."

"Please don't," one of his brothers added, but I couldn't tell which. It didn't sound like Brooks, though.

I snickered. "Nothing dirty. Camden put me in here to change. She wants to go to the pool."

"So you're in my room and getting naked. Please stay there and wait for me." The background began moving faster.

"Not a chance," I told him. "Sitting in the hot sun all day makes the pool too tempting."

Someone snorted and said, "Denied."

"Anyway. I thought you'd want to know I was here. Any secrets I should avoid?" I was teasing him more than anything.

First, any teenager-era secrets he had didn't matter to me.

And second, it'd been so long since he'd lived here, all of his things were probably gone. Other than the trophies.

"Not that I remember." His car door opened then closed, as did the other one, indicating one of his brothers was riding with him.

"Who's with you?" I asked because curiosity was a bitch.

"Urban." He moved the phone so that his brother took up the screen.

"Hey, Urban. How ya doing?" I hadn't seen him since he'd graduated the year before Cobb and I had. Or rather, seen him in person... in a personal way. I'd seen him play of course, but that had been on TV.

"Excellent, since Cobb and I kicked our older brothers' asses." Urban's dark hair was still damp from his aftergame shower, but he looked really good. They all always did.

Silas groaned. "It's only because you guys had Fraser."

"Keep telling yourself that, buddy." Urban clapped his back and Silas moved the phone so that I could only see him again. "Your catcher is getting old."

"I'll be sure to let Brooks know you think so."

This interaction reminded me of when they'd been kids. They'd always roasted each other and it was good to see that hadn't changed.

"Anyway…" Silas continued. "I have to drive. I'll be there in a bit."

"And I have to change," I told him before we said goodbye.

I didn't tell him that I loved him because I wasn't sure he wanted me to when his brother was right there. It was dumb. I was my own woman and should do what I wanted when I wanted. So I supposed I wasn't sure I *wanted* to say it in front of his brother.

Mostly because Silas hadn't said it back.

Ten minutes later, I was back downstairs with Camden and her mom, looking over the spread she'd had made for this cookout. The pool was enticing with its sparking waters, but we were going to eat first because she and I had decided our stomachs wouldn't last.

I'd put on my dark-blue two-piece suit. I didn't like calling it a "bikini" because it was in the old style. Not a string bikini and it had some coverage. Overtop that, I was wearing a white coverup that fastened at the side so it could pass for a dress. Camden was wearing something similar in white, though her bikini was slightly different.

That was when the guys all burst through the door as if they'd planned it.

First was Brooks and Cobb, then my dad and Diane, whom they said they'd met in the driveway. Then Mr. Briggs, and finally, Silas and Urban.

Silas came straight for me and didn't stop until he was close enough to push his hands into my hair while cupping my cheeks. Then without a word, he leaned down and kissed me. It wasn't meant to be much of a kiss, but everyone was there. Everyone was watching.

It meant something more than a kiss.

When he pulled back, I looked up at him. "You know everyone's right here."

The corners of his mouth turned up. "It's a statement."

Yeah, it was.

The room was quiet until he took a step away from me. Then everyone went about whatever they were doing.

Now there was no doubt to his family that we were together. We were public and he didn't care who knew.

We all ended up on the back patio, which wasn't really the word for it. Their backyard was a paradise only seen in dreams. Outside of the lush, green grass that I was sure they'd paid a bucket full to keep looking like that, there was a lot of concrete in the living area. One area that was attached to the house was covered with airflow on three sides and there was an outdoor kitchen where a woman was working away on the grill. There were a few other people working as well. Things were set up on a long countertop like a buffet and there was a large table big enough for probably twelve people.

Then there was the pool. It was a large rectangle filled to the top with water that looked like glass. When it got darker, the lights would come on and the place would look like we'd stepped into a Hawaiian night.

Over near the pool was what looked like an outdoor living room with furniture that was better than what I had in my apartment, but this was meant for the outdoors with cushions that I was sure someone removed when it stormed.

Everything was beautiful.

"I never got used to this back yard," I said right after we'd gotten out there.

"It's nice," said Silas.

I snorted. "Only someone who grew up here would call it 'nice.' This place is *gorgeous*. Jayce and I had a pretty cool playset when we were kids and my dad built that treehouse. That was *nice*. This… it's paradise."

"You want a back yard like this, I take it?" Cobb asked from beside me. The sons all looked alike. I'd gone to school with Cobb and we'd always been comfortable around each other. He was tall, though maybe an inch shorter than Silas, built about the same and had the dark hair with the dark, broody eyes. He was broodier than the others as well.

"I wish. I will never be able to afford anything close to this."

Cobb furrowed his brows and opened his mouth like he was about to say something, but Camden grabbed a hold of me. "We're getting food."

She was right. I was hungry.

This was the most laid-back I'd seen the family

in a long time. Even Mr. Briggs was laughing at something my dad had said—and no one saw him laugh much. But apparently, surrounded by the guys he'd roped into coaching the game, he was in his element.

I was finished eating and about to take my plate back over to the outdoor kitchen when a young woman appeared next to me and asked if she could take it. Talk about good service.

"So, Camden… when are you going to snag a baseball player?" I asked, which earned me a round of groans from her brother.

She acted like she was going to throw up. "Uh… never. I'll never date a baseball player. It's been a rule of mine and it's worked this long."

"I like that rule," Brooks said. A round of agreement went through the guys.

"Why?" I asked. "You're all baseball players.

"That's how we know," Urban offered.

"What's wrong with baseball players?" I was asking all of them, but not a one offered an answer until Camden spoke up.

"They're too full of themselves," she told me, which made me laugh. "They're so competitive. Nothing is ever good enough for them. They're gone so much and honestly, they're rarely ever faithful." She ticked it off like it was a list she had memorized until she got to the last one. Her eyes widened and she sat straight up.

"Jesus Christ, Camden," Brooks chided her, but I'd locked gazes with Silas.

Him cheating wasn't something I'd worried or thought about… until now.

The problem wasn't that she'd said it. The problem was that she wasn't wrong and I'd known that before we'd started this.

"Uh…" She hopped up and grabbed my hand. "Let's go in the pool."

I let her drag me up and quickly got rid of my coverup before she and I waded into the pool. I pulled my hair into a bun and secured it with an elastic I'd grabbed just for this. I didn't want to spend the rest of the night with soaking-wet hair.

She and I paddled ourselves to the other side, as far away from her brothers as we could get.

"I'm so sorry, Amity. I wasn't thinking when I spoke." She chewed the corner of her mouth. "I rarely do. It's a real problem."

"Don't worry about it. You didn't say anything that I didn't already know." Though I swallowed hard because I wished I didn't know it.

"I know, but… I shouldn't have said it. I didn't

mean Silas. I'm pretty sure you're it for him and he'd never hurt you."

Giving her my best unbothered smile, I said, "I know. I didn't think that." Which was only sort of a lie. There'd been a moment that it had flashed through my thoughts, but nothing more.

I had to trust Silas or this wouldn't work.

She bit her lips together then began moving away as someone slid in behind me so close that it could only be Silas.

"Sorry," she muttered again before swimming away.

Silas boxed me in with his arms, though I had enough room to turn to face him. At first, he just looked into my eyes until I rolled them and sighed.

"I'm fine. I didn't take what your sister said personally."

"*I* did," he countered. "I don't want you thinking that."

"What? That you're competitive and gone a lot?"

He gave me a fake smile that didn't even reach very far. "You know that's not what I'm talking about."

"I know. It's fine, Silas. Really. I'm not worried."

"You're not worried now, maybe, but you know I leave tomorrow."

My stomach tightened. He was right. He had a fucking road trip tomorrow. They were going to be gone seven days. A four-game series in one city and a three-game in the other.

"It's fine." I reached up to grab his shoulders so I could boost myself to kiss his cheek. "I'm fine. No worries."

And I'd do the best I could to make sure none of those worries that I'd just told him didn't exist *would* actually exist.

CHAPTER 20
SILAS

y sister and her fucking mouth.

Yeah, I knew that Camden hadn't meant anything by what she'd said and she'd just been answering the question about why she'd never date a ballplayer honestly.

But *fuck*.

I was about to be gone for a week and didn't want that to be on Amity's mind while I was away.

Cheating on Amity wasn't an option. First, regardless of what my sister thought of all players, I didn't cheat on anybody. Was that mostly because I avoided entanglements altogether? Could've been, but I'd always known that if I was with someone, I wouldn't hurt her like that.

Did a lot of the players cheat on their partners? Yeah.

But that wasn't me.

And I'd spent last night making sure Amity knew it, too. It'd been some of my best work. I'd fucked her until she'd said she wouldn't be able to walk today. At least she'd have that to remind her of me.

Seven days had never felt so long before.

I kissed her while she was still in bed intending to leave her there while I headed out. Since I'd left a key on the counter, I just told her to lock up when she left and the place was hers to use whenever she wanted to. The idea of her living there gave me all kinds of warm, fuzzy feelings, but I couldn't drop that then leave. She had her own place and I doubted she'd use mine, but I felt better knowing she could go there if she wanted to.

Yet before I could even get out the door, Amity rushed out, having thrown on clothes, and said she'd take me to the park so that my car didn't have to sit there for a week.

My gut told me to say *no* so I could continue to picture her all warm and cozy in my bed, but on the other hand, I wanted every second with her that I could get.

"Don't you work today?" I asked as I drove her Jeep through traffic. Normally, I would've just gotten in the passenger side, but she'd tossed me the key and said she was barely awake.

"I do." Amity covered a yawn that she couldn't hold back. "I'll take you, go home and shower, then go to work. My schedule is actually pretty flexible."

"Right." Now I'd be picturing her in the shower.

We pulled up to the park at the same time Jenner did and he stopped when we stepped out.

"I'm so disappointed in you, Amity." He stretched out his entire body right there on the street. It looked like he hadn't slept much last night, either. Wasn't a big deal. We had a game tonight, hence why we were leaving so early, but we could sleep on the bus and the plane.

"Fuck off," I told him, but it was full of humor. If anyone else had said that to her, it'd be a different story, but Jenner had been friends with her and her brother the same as I had. Or… hopefully not *exactly* the same because that, I'd have a problem with.

"What? I asked her to fuck with your head and she refused me."

Amity gave him a huge grin. "I didn't think it'd

work and I also didn't want to put myself in the path of Silas's anger."

"Whoa." I tugged her hand so she'd stop walking. "You told me about Jenner's *request*, but what the fuck are you talking about? My anger?"

Her smile faltered. "I didn't think anything I did would mess with your game. I didn't think I'd affect you."

"Because she didn't believe me," Jenner added, but I ignored that. I could address that with him later.

"My anger?" I asked her because that was the part I was really curious about.

"Yeah." She shrugged. "I've seen you angry. You charged at a pitcher during a game very recently."

"Yeah, that was to end—never mind. Doesn't matter. You know why I did that. But you..." I thrust my hand into her hair and stroked her cheek with my thumb. "Will never be in the path of my anger. I don't care how pissed I am."

Now, I knew she wasn't thinking I'd charge her like I had the pitcher. That wasn't what she was talking about at all. But for now, I had to go.

"That's my cue." Jenner slapped me on the back as he passed by. "I'll see you on the bus."

"You have to go," Amity said quietly.

"I do. I wish you were on this trip."

She tucked a piece of hair behind her ear. "Me too, but I think I'm going on the Florida trip. Peggy has other things on her schedule."

"Well, I'll see you in a week, but I'll call you later."

Before she could respond, I pinched her chin gently between my thumb and finger then leaned down to give my girl a kiss goodbye. The morning sun was so bright that I longed to be back in my dark bedroom with her warm body next to mine.

But for now, I had a job to do.

I'd savor this kiss, though, because it was going to be a long week.

"I have to go," I told her quietly once I'd ended the kiss. The corners of her mouth turned up.

"I'm not stopping you."

I snorted. "You kind of are." But I wasn't going to elaborate. Instead, I kissed her again quickly, made sure my bag was comfortable on my shoulder, and walked away from her.

I fucking hated doing it.

The sound a large group of grown men in a locker room wasn't unlike the sound of a middle school cafeteria with the exception of the fact that the voices were much deeper. It was loud and everyone was psyching everyone else up for the two series we had coming up.

Our manager would go over a few things before we got on the bus to the airport, but before that even happened, my dad appeared and waved me over.

He was the last person I wanted to deal with right now and if he weren't a legend in the sport and if his father-in-law hadn't owned the team, he wouldn't have been allowed in. When I got to him, he stepped out into the hall, so I did too while trying not to roll my eyes.

"Wanted to talk to you before you left."

"Go on, then." I waved my hand in the air so he'd hurry up.

"The girl was at the house last night, so I didn't get a chance to talk to you there."

I raised an eyebrow. "Amity." There was no doubt she was who he was talking about.

My dad wouldn't say anything *too* derogatory about her, not because she was my girl. No. That would warrant more shit talk, but because my mom would kill him and honestly, if Amity's dad found out, he'd go round for round with him.

Coach had never taken shit from my dad, no matter how much of a legend he was.

"Yeah. You don't bring girls to family things." He was right. I didn't.

"I mean… technically, Camden invited her."

Dad let out a sigh and shook his head. "That's bullshit. I saw you with her. You kissed her in front of everyone."

"I didn't know we were puritans now."

"We're not, but that girl is going to distract you from becoming the player you could be. That's what women do."

I narrowed my eyes on him. "Does Mom know you feel that way?"

He held up his hand. "Yes, but she was different."

"Because her dad owned a Major League team?"

His jaw tensed. That was a sore spot with him and we all knew it. It was why I'd said it.

Mom's dad had owned this team for decades. Probably before Dad had even played. Grandpa loved baseball, couldn't play himself at this level but had wanted to be involved. So he'd bought it because he'd already had more money than he could've used in three lifetimes. For years after

Mom and Dad had gotten together, there were rumors about why she was who Dad chose to settle down with..

Now, I knew my mom pretty well and she wouldn't be with my dad if she didn't love him. That wasn't her style.

Would my dad date, marry, and have a bunch of kids with a woman because it would further his agenda… *that*, I wasn't too sure about.

"Not because her dad owned a team, you little shit, but because she's different. She understood this game and what it takes to be the best."

"And you think Amity doesn't? Her dad is the best high school coach in the country. He's the reason any of your sons are playing at this level."

Another sore spot for my dad. He prided himself on passing the *talent* down to us himself and that had some truth to it. But if not for Coach, we wouldn't have known what to do with it. Dad sure as fuck hadn't spent the time with us developing those skills.

"That's not the same and you know it."

"I'm done here." I turned to walk away, but before I took a second step, Dad lowered the boom.

"You tell her the truth about her brother's accident?"

My chest tightened. No, I fucking hadn't and didn't really intend to, no matter how bad it made me feel.

After the accident, Coach had been there to console me, even though his only son had just died. He'd been adamant that he'd wanted to make sure Jenner and I had been all right. Even as he'd grieved, he'd assured me that he didn't blame me. That this had been an accident and it hadn't been my fault. He'd seen me spiraling and stepped in when he didn't have to. And he'd promised he'd never tell Amity.

A promise he'd stuck by.

What had my own dad done?

Made sure that I'd known it had been my fault Jayce had been out that night. That it had been my fault he'd been behind that wheel. That it had been my fault that he was dead.

I'd known it, but Dad had made sure I felt it in my core, where it would never be able to leave me.

"Didn't think so," he said when I didn't answer and also didn't turn back to him. "It was your fault her brother died. You don't think she's going to have feelings about that? You're comfortable fucking her, knowing she doesn't know the truth? Do you plan on *ever* telling her?"

After quickly wetting my lips, I turned back to him and took the number of steps needed to get close enough to him. Dad didn't intimidate me. I was actually a little taller than him and since I was in my prime and he was getting older, he didn't physically pose a threat of any kind.

"You need to keep your mouth shut about that."

This stupid, shitty grin appeared. "Honesty is the bedrock of any relationship." He turned and left as if he didn't have a care in the world, while I'd never wanted to punch my father so badly in my life.

Now I had hours on a bus then a plane to think about what he'd said.

And the fact that he wasn't wrong.

My dad's voice echoed in my thoughts the entire trip and I was barely able to focus once we'd arrived, but I had to push it and Amity out of my mind.

I had some games to win.

Unfortunately, as I lay in the bed in the hotel that night, I wasn't so successful. I'd had a good game, wanted to call Amity but hadn't. She was going to hate me when she found out that everything my dad said was true.

I'd gotten her brother killed.

So I didn't call her that night.

Or the next.

I still got texts from her saying *good morning* or *good night* or *I miss you* and I read every one of them. Yet I didn't answer a single thing.

I went the week without talking to her and eventually, those little texts stopped. I did get one from my sister asking me what the fuck I was doing, which meant she'd been talking to Amity, but I ignored her too.

It was a shitty thing to do, but my focus was hanging by a thread and I couldn't fuck up my entire life. My career might be the only thing I had left.

Finally, after seven games on the road, we were back in Kalamazoo and had a night game. We hadn't traveled far enough to warrant a day off when we got back. Though when we arrived back at our baseball field, it felt a lot less like coming home. Especially because this time, Amity wasn't there to welcome me.

We did our warmup and were back in the clubhouse when Brooks dropped into his chair next to mine. "What the fuck is wrong with you?" he asked.

"Don't know what you're talking about." But I did.

"You do." *Fuck.* He knew me too well. "You haven't been yourself since we went on the road. You're playing fine, but fuck… something's off and trust me when I tell you that I wish I didn't know that, but I know you too well."

We were only two years apart, so he'd been there for every fucking thing. He'd been the one who'd made sure I'd known how to use a condom when I'd been about to have sex for the first time. I'd already known, but watching him put one on a banana had been too good to pass up.

"Nothing."

"You see Amity when we came in?"

I shook my head slowly.

"Ah. So that's it. Go find your girl and an empty room to blow the cobwebs out of you. *Fuck.* Do *something* to get you over whatever this is."

I couldn't do that and I wasn't about to tell him. Before I could figure out a lie as to why I couldn't do that, there was a loud knock on the clubhouse door. That usually happened when someone who didn't normally belong here was about to come in and wanted to make sure there weren't dicks flapping in the wind.

Martins over by the door called out, "Come in."

The door opened and Amity walked through it

wearing a summer dress that stopped just above her knees. It hugged her waist then flared out but was tight against her top half. There were short sleeves and her hair was up, yet there were little pieces that had come loose from the bun.

She was damned beautiful and I'd missed the fuck out of her while we'd been gone.

Her gaze locked on mine and while I wanted to believe it was a palpable heat, it was really anger and she had every right to it.

Amity quickly wet her lips and looked away from me. "Jimenez, I need to see you for a minute."

I was jealous of the fucker because he was going to be close to her and it probably had to do with his travel documents or a form that needed to be updated. Amity did that a lot.

"Fuck," Brooks ground out, though it sounded like he was trying not to laugh. "You're fucked. That woman is *pissed*. What'd you do?"

"I don't think he called her while we were gone," Jenner told him.

My brother let out a loud laugh. "Oh, you are fucked. Why the hell would you do that? I know you know better, even if you've never had to put it into practice."

"You can both fuck off."

I watched that door like it was the one paying my salary. As soon as Jiminez came back, I bolted.

"Go," Brooks called after me. "Grovel. See if she'll forgive you." Then he and Jenner laughed again.

I didn't care about him. I cared about her.

The worst part of all this was that my dad had been right. It would've been better to never get involved with anyone. She and I should've been friends and nothing more, but at this point, I couldn't go back.

Maybe I wasn't going to be with her because I had fucked up, but I also couldn't be friends with her after this. Not when I knew how she tasted and the tiny sounds she made when she came. I wouldn't be able to *not* think of those things.

"Amity," I called out, but she kept walking, so I hurried my steps. "Amity." When I got to her, I grabbed her arm so she'd stop. When she did, I slid around the other side of her so we'd be face to face because it'd been clear she wasn't going to look at me.

"Is there something you need?" she asked, avoiding looking into my eyes. Suddenly, the papers in her hand were very interesting to her. When I didn't answer right away, she said,

"Silas?" Then sighed. "Look, I have work to do."

She slid past me to keep moving, but I stood in her way.

I had no idea what was going through my brain at that moment.

She was angry and hot as hell. I hadn't seen her in a week, and I was probably going to break her heart by telling her the truth, yet none of the words would form and I had a game that I had to get to.

Instead of telling her any of that or that I loved her, I cupped her face and tilted it back, kissing her like she was the only oxygen in the concourse.

Her body was rigid at first then she pushed me away.

"I work here, Silas."

"Yeah. Me too." I glanced around and found exactly where I was going to take her so no one else would see this. "Come on."

Amity came with me willingly and while I knew it was the wrong thing to do—she was right. She worked here. Still, I was determined to have this.

I needed to be with her one last time before I told her the truth.

CHAPTER 21
AMITY

*S*ilas pulled me into this storage room off the concourse, which reminded me of the room in New York where we'd first had sex. But I was angry. He hadn't explained why he'd just ignored me for a week and I'd given in to that kiss on the concourse because I'd wanted it so badly.

"Are you going to explain?" I asked him because that was what I really wanted. However, me being mad didn't change the fact that it'd also been a week since he'd touched me and I'd quickly grown addicted to it.

"I don't have time. I have a game." He leaned in to kiss me again, but I turned my head so his mouth would land on my cheek.

"Then we'll talk later."

"We will." He started to slip his hand up the outside of my thigh, pushing my dress with it.

I hated the fact that my stomach did a somersault and desire pooled inside me. I was mad. My stupid body didn't seem to care.

"Then we'll do this later too." There was a brief moment I considered acting like I was going to push him away, but even I couldn't pretend that. I wanted him close, craved his touch. The aroma of his soap even turned me on at this point.

Silas traced his nose over my jaw then kissed my neck before burying his face there. It was like he just wanted to be close to me too.

"I'm mad at you." My words came out breathy because every single thing he did affected me.

"I know." His breath feathered against my skin and I would've sworn it traveled down the backs of my legs, making my knees consider buckling.

Well… I could be mad at him and still have sex, right?

It might've been wrong, but I was going to do it anyway.

Quickly, I pulled the hem of his shirt out from his pants. He was still in his practice stuff and not his uniform and I didn't stop until I yanked his shirt over his head. We wouldn't get fully naked in this room that anyone could've come into, but I wanted access to his chest and back.

Silas's head popped up. I brought him down so that I could kiss him. Normally, it was either he was kissing me or we were kissing each other, but here, now, *I* was kissing *him*. And he was letting me.

The kisses were brutal. Anger came out in everything I did and it seemed like he was mad about something too, but it couldn't have been me because I hadn't done anything.

We didn't have much time.

Those kisses became like stolen, desperate moments we had while we were running on a clock because we were. Silas backed us up until my legs hit a table, then he lifted. All without breaking our connection.

He pushed my thighs apart and ran his fingers over my panties before pulling them aside and touching me where I ached for him. I didn't let him touch me for too long before I was undoing his belt and unzipping his pants.

His thick, hard cock sprung free, like it'd been waiting all day for me to do that. Then I moved myself to the end of the table and lined him up. He took the hint.

Silas thrust into me in one motion. I was more

than ready for him. He nipped at my ear and kissed down to my chest then sucked gently at the swells of my breasts. We didn't have long and after a week, this wouldn't take long.

When his thumb brushed my clit, it was all the encouragement I needed. My body lit up like Fourth of July fireworks as my orgasm overtook me. He followed right after like he'd been holding out and waiting for me. Maybe he had been.

After, he pulled out of me and righted my panties then shoved himself back into his pants. Looked like a stop at the restroom was the next order of business for the both of us.

Did that count as angry sex? I had definitely been angry.

"Can you at least tell me why you didn't respond to any of my texts?" I asked as I hopped off the table. "I don't like feeling clingy and you kind of had me feeling that way." I took a breath. If I wanted him to be honest with me, then I had to be with him, right? "You had me worried about things I shouldn't have to worry about."

His jaw tightened. "Like?"

I swallowed hard. This was likely to piss him off, but he'd asked. "Like maybe you were with someone else. You spent the night before you left making sure I was secure in the fact that you wouldn't cheat on me after what Camden had said. Then you fucking disappear on me for a week."

"'Disappear'?" he snapped and I didn't love the tone in his voice. "The games are televised. You could see me every day."

I scoffed. "You know that's not what I'm talking about, Silas. A quick goodnight text would've sufficed. Did Camden get in your head?"

"Camden, my dad. Fucking everyone has an opinion."

I snapped back. "So you're mad at me because your family oversteps? I don't control that."

He leaned down so he was at my eye level and it felt vaguely condescending when he spoke slowly. "I don't have time to do this right now. I have a game."

"Then why did you bring me in here? If you're so strapped for time, you didn't need to do me any favors."

"This wasn't about *you*," he yelled, making me take two steps away from him. Not the yelling. The guys yelled and were loud all of the time. But the idea that what we'd just done hadn't been about me? No. I wasn't accepting that. It hadn't *all* been about me, but it had been a little bit.

"What is going on with you?" There was something he wasn't telling me and now was the time for him to be out with it. This was too big of a change from a week ago.

"Nothing."

"Don't tell me *nothing*. You are not acting like the same person who went on a road trip a week ago." The blood in my body turned cold at what might've made him do a turnaround. "Did something happen on the road?"

"No," he snapped again. "If you think I'd cheat on you, then what are we even doing here?"

Somehow, that didn't make me feel much better. "Then tell me why you're angry with me. I know why I am with you and so do you. I deserve the same."

He sighed. "Now isn't the time." He wet his lips. "I'm not mad at you." Sure as hell could've fooled me. "I killed your brother." My world tilted to the side and I was going to fall over. "Or at least I'm the reason he's dead. I didn't want to tell you. I'm fucking pissed at myself."

My breath quickened and my heart thudded against my chest and in my ears. "What?"

He reached out to touch me, but I stepped

away. My eyes burned with tears that I was no doubt going to let fall.

"Why are you saying that?" I asked because in my mind, it couldn't be true.

My brother had died in an accident. This didn't make sense.

Silas ran a hand over his face as if he were trying to wipe away the regret. "I don't have time for this, Amity."

I was stunned and my brain wasn't working right as he moved past me to the door. As if he were going to drop this huge bomb and leave me standing here.

But if he… if he'd gotten my brother killed… and he'd hidden that fact, there wasn't really anything left to say. Camden had told me he had survivor's guilt. That wasn't what it sounded like to me.

"Is that why you never told me you loved me?" I asked, quietly bringing him to a stop before he opened the door. "Did you never love me or did you just not want to say it?"

"I did tell you." He turned to face me. "I told you over and over and over the only way I know how."

"You didn't. You didn't say the words. To me, that means you don't."

He wet his bottom lips slowly. "You see what you want to see, Amity."

And then he left me standing in that room that smelled like sex and his soap, as if I were just another woman he could toss aside.

My sanity was threatening to break and I had to get out of here.

Vowing not to let myself cry was the only thing that kept me from doing it. After a quick stop in the restroom, I went to my boss and told her I had a family emergency. One look at my face and she told me to go.

I couldn't work right now anyway.

And I knew exactly where I needed to go.

I needed my dad.

It was afternoon, which meant it was before his game after school. So to the school I went. The secretary at the front desk knew me, so she buzzed me in before I could hit the button, then she waved as I passed the office to head to my dad's office near the gym.

Dad was inside at his desk going over what was probably the lineup for his game today. They were on the road to the playoffs and he wouldn't stop until he was happy with every detail.

A quick tap on his open door brought his attention to me.

Dad furrowed his brows as he quickly pushed up from his chair.

"Honey, what are you doing here?" He didn't stop until he was in front of me.

"I need to talk to you."

"Come in." He gently pulled me in then shut the door behind him before leading me over to the chair next to his desk. Then he took his seat and rolled it over in front of me. "What's going on?"

"Why did Silas just tell me that he killed Jayce?"

Dad's eyes shut tightly and his jaw tensed. "Because he feels responsible, but he didn't kill your brother. It was an accident."

A tear from each eye broke loose and ran down my cheek. Dad reached out to gently brush them away.

"If it was an accident, then… is Silas telling me that because he doesn't want to be with me? Is it an easy out for him? There has to be a reason."

Dad sat back and sighed. It wasn't an annoyed sound, but the one he made when the subject of my brother came up and we both knew it was going to be a painful conversation.

"He feels like he's responsible because… he was the reason Jayce was in Silas's car driving that night."

"I don't understand." My cheeks were wetter than I'd expected when I swiped a hand under each side. "Make it make sense, Dad."

"They were kids being kids," he said, as if that made any sense. "Silas and Jenner had been at a party. They were drinking and Silas was still going to drive home. He said he told Jayce that he was fine."

"Was Jayce there?" I asked. "Was he drinking?"

Dad shook his head. "Jayce was at home until he got texts from friends saying he should come get Silas and Jenner. So he went. Had a friend drop him off so he wouldn't have to leave his car." It had never made sense to me that Jayce had been driving Silas's car and not his own but I avoided talking about the accident as much as possible to protect myself and my dad. "Silas and Jenner said they gave Jayce a hard time about leaving, but your brother got them out of there before it got worse. It was really late. Dark. They weren't in the city and while no one really knows because the two eye witnesses were drunk sixteen-year-olds, the police said it looked like Jayce swerved to miss something. Maybe an animal. Lost control of the car and… well, you know what happened from there.”

Suddenly, Dad looked at least ten years older than he had when we'd started this conversation.

“So he feels responsible because he was stupid for drinking the way he had. He and Jenner were the reason your brother was out on the road. So in his mind, he's the reason your brother died. Jenner processed it in a different way. But I told Silas to get counseling back then, but I don't think Conrad actually let him.” Dad scratched the back of his head. “I thought that maybe since he was with you, he'd gotten past all of that.”

“You were wrong,” my watery voice told him and the dam broke.

Dad took me in his strong arms and let me cry, soaking his shirt to his skin. I was crying because Silas and I had just broken up. I was crying because my brother was dead and it had been a stupid, possibly avoidable accident.

“Is this why Jenner and Silas put distance between me and them after the funeral?” They'd still been around, but not like when my brother had been alive.

When he'd been alive, they'd check on me themselves. Sit at a table in the cafeteria with me if they'd actually been eating in there. They'd made me feel like they'd been my friends, too.

"Probably," he said, then he kissed my forehead. "I'm going to have my assistant coach take over today. We can go home and talk some more."

"No." I didn't want to interrupt what he had going on. Instead, I wiped my tears away and put on a brave face. "You do your game. I'd come, but…" That was an understatement. "I'm just going to go home and wallow for a while."

"Which is what I *don't* want you to do."

"I'll call Camden. We'll go get some food or order in or something." I patted his back. "Go to your game. There are a bunch of future professional players counting on you."

Though I knew that if I gave even the smallest indication of needing him, Dad would have walked away from the game in an instant. He'd always made it clear that he loved his job and it was important to him, but that was a distant second to how important I was.

"Are you sure? I really don't mind."

"I'm sure, Dad. We can get together tomorrow. You don't have a game."

With reluctance, he let me leave that office without taking the game off.

When I got to my car, I pressed Camden's name in my contacts and she answered on the second ring.

"Are you going to the game tonight?" I asked her without saying *hello*.

"I planned to, but if you're not…"

"I'm not. Want to meet at Cleats & Kegs?"

"I'm already on my way."

I chose to go to the bar instead of home because I knew that once I got to the comfort of my house, I'd let all my emotions run all over me and I'd be a puddle on the carpet.

I wasn't ready for that yet.

Right now, I wanted some female camaraderie, a little girl talk in which maybe we'd plan all the ways I could castrate Silas while leaving him alive.

As you did when your heart had just been crushed.

CHAPTER 22
AMITY

I was sitting in my car in the parking lot of a high school contemplating whether I was really going to lean on my boyfriend's sister for support due to damage her brother had done.

Oh. Sorry. Ex-boyfriend.

Apparently, I only saw what I wanted to see.

It wasn't the first time he'd said that to me, but I had the suspicion that it'd be the last.

Leaning on Camden seemed unfair to me. Her loyalty should have been to her brother. But she was the only female friend I had in town whom I could talk to. Harper could be trusted, but we weren't there yet. Camden had quickly become my best friend. I might not have been hers, but she was mine.

When I pulled up to Cleats & Kegs, I thought about texting her that I was just going to go home, but since I'd called her out here, I couldn't do it.

Once inside, I scanned the room. It was early, so the place wasn't busy yet. There were a few people on one side enjoying what might've been the best burger in Kalamazoo. And there were others also eating, maybe having a drink, I didn't know.

I also didn't care.

It'd start to pick up soon due to people coming for the game and wanting to grab a bite before they did. It was part of the reason this place was successful.

The music was lower than it was later in the evening when this place was a full-on bar full of drunk people and if I were being honest, I'd want the noise to drown the people out at that time as well. For now, we could all mind our own business.

I chose the booth farthest back near the kitchen entrance and the restrooms. It was where Camden and I typically sat. No one would bother us back there.

"Hey, hon," Harlowe slid up with her blonde hair pulled into a bun, though there were tiny wisps that had escaped. She'd probably already been working all day. There was no uniform that I knew of because she always wore jeans and a snug-fitting T-shirt that she filled out much better than I would have. "Camden coming?"

I nodded. "Should be here any minute."

"Excellent. I'll grab you both a diet then have them start burgers." It wasn't a question, but if I was going to eat here, it'd be burgers.

I just didn't think I'd eat much.

Harlowe waved toward the door, which made me look over to see Camden hurrying toward me. She had her dark hair down and it was wavy and she was wearing shorts and a tank top as I would've expected her to be if she'd planned on going to the game.

"What'd my brother do?" she asked before sliding into the booth where I was sitting.

"You're dressed for the game," I told her. "You can go. I'll just take my burger home."

Camden rolled her eyes. "What'd my brother do?"

"Why do you think he did something?" I'd hoped she wouldn't see it on my face, but she had me suspecting otherwise.

"Please." She scoffed. "It's written all over your face and also I called him like ten minutes before you called me. To say he was less than pleasant would be an understatement."

I furrowed my brows. What gave him the right to be pissy? He was the one who'd dropped a bomb on me then brushed off the love talk and once again told me that I only saw what I wanted to. "What do you mean?"

"First, he answered the phone with a very short '*What?*' Normally, if he answers me, it's more of an 'Oh, my bratty sister is calling me, how annoying' tone. Then I didn't even get to ask him the question that I wanted to ask before he said he had to go and hung up on me." She took a long drink from the pop that Harlowe had just dropped off. "Like… my brothers can be fucking assholes, but usually, they aren't so bad to me. And he was a fucking asshole. So…" She waved her hand in front of me to indicate that I should start talking.

I too took a drink because my mouth was suddenly dry.

"I saw him at the stadium earlier. He seemed angry but I was because he'd ignored me all week." I swallowed hard. "I wasn't asking for much, I didn't think. Just a good night text or something. Like I understand what his job is."

She set her cup onto the table harder than she needed to. "He didn't just come right out and apologize? Why would he do that?" Then her eyes grew wide. "Did he say it was because of what I said at my parents' house? About not dating players because they're cheaters?"

I shrugged. "I told him I wasn't worried about it."

Camden leaned in close. "But were you a little worried?"

That was something that needed an honest answer and I didn't want to give it, but it was what I'd asked her here for.

"Not really," I told her. "I mean, I've always known there's a chance. My brother played baseball in high school. I saw up close what they're like. And that was high school. But no. I wasn't really worried until he didn't talk to me."

"Then… what?"

"I don't know what set it off." But still, I recapped everything that had happened when I'd seen her brother earlier. The argument. The sex, though I left out the details. Everything he'd said before he'd walked away from me. If she was going to be there to support me, she needed to know all of it. I'd be there for her in a similar situation in a heartbeat.

"That fucking idiot."

"I don't know," I told her. "Maybe some of it's my fault? Like I knew he had survivor's guilt about my brother. Maybe I should've pushed him to tell me about it."

"No." She held her hand up to stop me. "We're not going to do that. We aren't going to take their shit on as our own. He's a grown man. He could've told you what had really happened at any point and he chose not to. That's not on you."

Harlowe dropped off our burgers, but my stomach was in knots, so I was just going to nibble on the fries.

"I know. My dad told me, though. Why Silas thinks it's his fault that my brother is dead." I shook my head as the memory of those first days tried to creep in. I couldn't handle going there right now. "It was an accident. A stupid accident."

"Silas never really let go, ya know?" she asked and I didn't know what she was talking about. "In high school. My dad rode the guys hard. Still does." She lowered her voice to mimic her father's. "'You've got to be the best. If you're not the best, then you're the worst.'"

"Jesus Christ," I muttered.

"Yeah. So the guys figured out ways to let off steam and"—she gagged, like she really didn't want to say what was coming next—"most of them, I assumed, used girls to do that. But none of them really let go. They didn't do the whole drinking scene and the other shit you see in high school. None of them smoked weed because could you imagine if they'd gotten caught?"

Yeah. I could and it wouldn't have been pretty.

"So… if the one time Silas let loose, your brother has the accident… I can see why Silas would say it's his fault. He wouldn't want it to be your brother's."

"It was an accident." Meaning it wasn't anyone's fault.

"Listen." She took a big bite of the juicy burger and swallowed it before continuing. "I never said my brothers were rational."

"Well." I sat up straighter and decided that I too would eat the damn burger. "I can understand all of that, but none of it gives him the right to make me feel the way he did."

"Of course not."

"So, I'm going to take this as a learning opportunity and never date a ballplayer again."

"Welcome to the club."

But there was still one thing bothering me and since I'd told her everything else, I could tell her this. "The thing is… we had sex in that room and it was completely consensual. I was angry and it was angry sex—"

"Which can be so, so good… I hear."

I snorted. "It can be, but it also made me feel… *used* isn't the right word, but it was like he fucked me knowing that he was going to walk away when it was done. I didn't realize it until it was over, of course."

"If you would've known he was going to walk away after, would you still have done it?"

That was probably the easiest question to answer. "Yes," I said immediately. "But at least then I'd know it was the last time."

"Well, then, it wasn't a waste."

We ate our burgers while changing the subject to something much more fun, which could've been the latest discoveries in algebra, as far as fun went. It wasn't until the table was cleared and we'd been there too long that something else occurred to me.

"There's still the Florida trip," I told her. "I can't back out. Peggy has already made plans, so I have to go and he'll be there, of course. How in the hell do I handle seeing him after all of this?"

Camden took a deep breath and folded her arms one over the other on the tabletop. "The same way you did it when you were in love with him, but he didn't know it. You just do it. We're strong women. No fucking way is some guy going to ruin anything for us. Not our jobs, anyway."

And she was right. I had to go on that trip and act like everything was fine. Professional. I'd avoid him otherwise.

"Want me to go too?" she asked. Since she wasn't in school right now and her parents had more money than a person could use in several lifetimes, Camden could hop a flight to Florida at the drop of a hat. Plus, it was her brother Urban's team. She could see him while she was there.

"You don't have to do that," I told her, but deep down, I wanted her to. It wasn't something I could ask for, though, because talk about interrupting a person's life.

She set her phone down, which I hadn't really noticed her pick it up in the first place. "I'm going. I just sent my mom a text asking her to make all of the arrangements. Or, rather, asking her to have her assistant make all of the arrangements."

What a life to lead where you could just snap your fingers and things happened.

"Thank you, Camden. You didn't have to do that, but I'm so glad that you did."

At least I'd have one friend in Florida.

CHAPTER 23
SILAS

Three fucking days.

It'd been three days since I'd talked to Amity or *fuck*. Seen her. She was either really busy or doing everything in her power to avoid me.

I'd told her dad that she'd be pissed if she knew the truth and I'd been right.

She hated me.

And I wasn't sure if her hating me was worth the time I'd gotten with her.

Who was I kidding? It was. I'd give anything up to have the memory of those days, even though I'd always known, deep down, it would be temporary. Amity was eventually going to learn the truth about her brother's accident and the fact that it had been my fault he'd been out there in the first place, so it'd always be over. Fuck, Jenner had only gone out with me that night because I'd basically forced him to.

I'd been good while it had lasted, though.

"What the fuck's wrong with you?" Jenner asked as he tossed his glove into his locker. The lockers weren't like traditional lockers. They were more like cubbies, but I felt five years old referring to them that way. They were large and open with a chair in front of it. It was a place for our things when we were in the clubhouse.

"Not a fucking thing," I snapped. I'd been snapping at everyone for days and no one could pretend that I wasn't lying with that answer.

"The fuck there isn't." Brooks came out of the shower right then with an already-forming bruise on his chest from the hard hit of someone sliding into home. He was the most battered player on the team. "You've been a fucking asshole for days. Amity still pissed?"

I clenched my jaw at the mention of her and my chest tightened. But now was as good of a time as any to tell them. "We're not together. But yeah, I assume she's pissed at me."

"What the fuck did you do?" Jenner asked, but it was under his breath, as if he didn't fully mean for me to hear it.

Brook stood up straight. "Did you fuck someone else?"

I raised my middle finger at him, but it was only halfhearted. It would've been easier if I had fucked someone else on that road trip. That was an easier to handle reason for Amity to hate me. "I didn't fuck someone else. Fuck off. I wouldn't do that."

His face pinched up, like he didn't fully believe me. "Then what the fuck did you do for her to still be so pissed? That girl has had feelings for you since she was, what? Thirteen, maybe? We all knew it. Which means you had to do something pretty terrible to get her so angry that she's not talking to you. You didn't call her and that was a major fuckup, but I'd think you'd know how to make that better."

"I told her it's my fault Jayce is dead."

Brooks groaned. "Not with that shit again."

"I was there, too," Jenner added and he had been. He'd been drinking too, but it hadn't been anything new to him. He'd done that sometimes, but he'd never had to be rescued from a situation before that night and he'd only been there because I pushed him to go. Jayce rejected my pressure and told me I was an asshole for going to that party before I'd even left.

"It was an accident, man," Brooks continued, as if Jenner hadn't spoken. "Get some therapy or something, but get over it. Or get past it. Whatever I'm supposed to say. But don't let it cost you the only woman you've ever cared about."

I pushed up from my chair, angrily sending it back into my locker. "She doesn't want to see me." I couldn't put it any plainer than that. "It's done. Get over it."

Brooks's eyes widened, but he grinned. "Oh, I'm already fucking over it. Your relationships are yours to fuck up." He came close to me, like he would've if I were someone he was trying to intimidate. But none of the brothers intimidated the other. "But I also don't want to hear your bitching when she's with someone else. If you're going to be a pussy here, then you don't deserve to have her in the first place."

I clenched my fists at my sides. Hitting my brother wasn't something I was going to do, especially in the clubhouse, but fuck, I wanted to.

Mostly because he was right and I was too thickheaded to admit it.

"Whoa." Jenner slid between the two of us, causing both of us to take a step back. "Maybe everyone should calm down. Tensions are high. We lost today and that fucking sucks."

"Yeah, I wonder why we lost," Brooks muttered.

"What's that supposed to mean?" I asked, but I already knew.

"Uh, that you're playing like shit. I thought that was clear."

Jenner put a hand on my chest when I went to step forward. I needed out of this clubhouse and now. I was already showered and changed. It was time to go.

"You can go to hell, Brooks." Then I grabbed my duffle and headed for the door.

I didn't stop when Jenner called my name. He wouldn't follow me. Both he and my brother were only wearing towels and that would've broken all kinds of rules.

My car was in sight when I saw something move out of the corner of my eye. My gut told me not to ignore it.

It was Amity walking across the parking garage, I assumed to her car. She was looking down at her phone, which I wanted to tell her wasn't the safest way for a woman to walk through a parking garage, but I couldn't. She didn't see me standing there like a fucking stalker.

The skirt of her dress slapped against her legs as she made her way down the aisle. Her hair was down and moving in the gentle breeze. My fingers begged to thread themselves into it, but she wasn't mine anymore and I couldn't do that.

Her bag went into her car first, then she climbed in behind it.

It was the first morsel of Amity I'd had since I'd left her in that storage room in the stadium.

And it left me harder than I'd ever been in my life.

Two more shitty games later and we were boarding a plane for Florida. I was already on board pretending not to be watching every person who came on, waiting to see Amity. She'd said she'd be on this trip before. We'd had different plans for Florida then, but I'd still at least get to see her.

Only she wasn't on the plane yet and it had my stomach in knots.

Then, right when I thought the flight attendant was going to pull the door closed, Amity hurried on. She gave the woman a grateful smile then slid into a seat in the first row without looking around. She was wearing slightly loose cropped pants—the kind that rolled at the bottom but only went to mid-calf —as well as sandals and a T-shirt.

We were required to dress up for travel, but she clearly wasn't. She still looked sexy as hell and I knew that I couldn't be the only one who thought that.

Amity was objectively beautiful on the outside, but once you got to know her… she was breathtaking.

And I'd fucked it up.

Since she was the last person on the plane and sat near the front, Amity shot off the airplane like her ass was on fire as soon as the door opened.

Fuck. She really wanted to avoid my ass. With all of this, the last thing I wanted to do was affect her job, which meant I was going to have to talk to her. Apologize for the way I'd left things. After all, I could've handled that so much better. The result would've been the same, but maybe it wouldn't be affecting her job.

I didn't know.

"You should go after her, man." Jenner slapped me on the back as he spoke.

"Mind your business," I told him because it was taking everything in my power not to do just that. "She clearly doesn't want to talk to me."

"And that's going to stop you?"

Yeah. It was at least for now because I didn't

want to be in her space when she didn't want me there.

The team loaded up onto a bus to go from the plane to the ballpark. We had a game tonight.

It took a lot of effort, but I put that woman out of my mind and actually got some hits. This was more like me. The series at home, my head hadn't been in the game when I'd needed it to be.

Camden was in the stands on Urban's side of the field, which made me laugh. She was showing her support and I had to think that she knew what had happened between Amity and me.

But I wanted to know for sure.

"Camden," I called out after the game ended and most people had filed out of their seats. My sister looked back then let out a big sigh. Her whole body was into it. Then she came down the few stairs until she was by the field. But she didn't come over to the visitors' side.

Urban met the two of us there.

"Hey, big brother," he said with his arms out. I reciprocated and gave him a hug.

Urban looked more like Cobb than anyone. It was like he and Cobb had been meant to be twins, but Mom had them a year apart. Then again, we all looked related, so what did I know?

"Good game," I told him because it had been. It'd been a battle to win.

"Yeah. Yeah." He played first base and whenever I'd gotten a single, or Brooks had, or hell, Jenner, we'd given him shit. I'd been so into it that I'd almost gotten thrown out.

"It was a good game," Camden added. "I expect tomorrow to have me on the edge of my seat."

Urban snorted. "I'll do my best."

Camden turned to me. "Did you want something?"

I glanced at Urban then back to her. Him being there hadn't been part of my plan, but he was family and I wanted answers.

"What do you know?" I asked her without going into more detail.

Camden narrowed her eyes and pursed her lips before taking a deep breath. "I know lots of things, big brother. Care to be more specific?"

"Camden," I said through clenched teeth.

"Yeah. I know. She's pissed."

"Are we talking about Amity?" Urban asked as he watched the two of us go back and forth.

I slid my gaze over to him and he held up his hands.

"Camden keeps me well informed."

Of course she did. Then again, secrets had never been a big thing between the siblings. If something happened, we all knew it.

"Camden," I said much more nicely.

"What?" She threw her hands in the air, like she was frustrated with me. "What do you want to know? But I should warn you, Amity is my friend and there are things I'm not going to tell you."

Yeah. Of course. "Look." I moved closer to her. "I just want to know that she's all right. That this shit isn't going to interfere with her job."

Camden snorted. It was a family thing, I supposed. "She's not *all right*. She had her heart broken by some thickheaded guy. But no. I don't see her allowing it to impact her job. She loves working for the team. That doesn't change because one of them turns out to be an asshole."

"Ouch," Urban offered. "We can all be assholes, though."

Camden raised an eyebrow. "Do you all also have sex with a woman at her job in a room where anyone could've walked in when you knew you were going to crush her heart after?" When Urban didn't answer, she rolled her eyes. "This is why I won't date ballplayers."

Some of those details could've been skewed because I'd hurt her, but Amity wasn't totally wrong. I had done that because I'd selfishly wanted one last time with her.

"I'm going to go shower," Urban said as he backed away like Camden was a bomb waiting to explode. "We're still going to dinner, right?"

"Yeah." But I didn't take my eyes off my sister.

"You know…" Now she leaned in closer to me. "You would be in such a better place if you would've just talked to her. Talked. Which would've included some listening. Now…" She shook her head. "I think you've missed your chance to fix it."

Fuck.

That meant Amity had told her it was too late. Not that I would've been able to fix it, anyway.

Once we were all showered and dressed, we took the bus to the hotel. I dropped my bag in my room then met Brooks and Camden in the lobby, where Urban picked us up. This was where he lived, so he knew the area and was driving us.

We had a nice dinner, only missing Cobb, and while I loved being with my siblings, my mind was somewhere else completely. It was on the third floor of the hotel where Amity's room was. Her being in there alone on this trip hurt.

The idea that maybe she wasn't alone filled me with a fury that I wasn't entitled to.

When we got back to the hotel, I waited until Brooks's door shut. Camden had to go to another floor because she wasn't with the team and that was where the hotel had put her.

Now that I was alone, I headed to Amity's room. Camden had let is slip which was her and I didn't know if it was accidental or not but I was thankful.

First, I knocked lightly. There was movement in the room and the floor on the other side of the door creaked.

She was on the other side, likely pushing up to her toes to look out the peephole.

But she didn't open the door.

I knocked again.

This time, I was met with silence.

Probably for the best. Seeing her would remind me of what I was going to miss for the rest of my life. It'd remind me that I was the reason she had the most painful memory of her life.

If she could live with being around me for her job, I wasn't going to push her.

The next day had me rethinking that.

Amity sat next to Camden in the stands, this time, near the visitors' dugout.

I knew she could see every time that I looked at her, but she didn't make eye contact with me and ignored me. She at least looked like she was having a good time. She and Camden were laughing and joking and cheering…

But Amity didn't cheer for me. She was all in every time someone else did something, but when I smacked a home run, Camden leaped from her seat, but Amity stayed put and acted like she hadn't noticed.

I rounded the bases then was back in the dugout.

"Oh, you're fucked," Brooks told me, but there was too much humor in his voice. Not that I blamed him. I'd sound the same way if the situation had been reversed.

"Yeah," I agreed. "I am."

That didn't mean I wouldn't give it one last shot when we got back to Michigan.

If for no other reason than to apologize to her.

I at least owed her that.

Florida was a fucking nightmare.

Not only was it unbearably hot and humid—and that was coming from someone from Michigan where, in the summer, the heat and humidity could get so high that it felt like you were chewing air—but it took a lot of effort on my part to act like being around Silas didn't affect me.

When clearly, it did.

In the time since our blowup in at the baseball park, I'd talked to my dad more and to Camden. I'd been able to work through my feelings about everything he'd said and I knew one thing for sure.

Silas may have been there, but my brother's accident had been just that. An accident.

Now, I could've gone to him and tried to

convince him and made sure he knew that I didn't blame him, but with the way he'd spoken to me and the other things he'd said… I wasn't so sure I wanted to do that.

Not to mention many others had tried to reason with him about his guilt over the accident and it had never worked. There was no reason to believe that anything I said would make a difference in a meaningful way.

It definitely could've ended up with more hurt feelings for me.

"Amity," a voice called out to me after I'd boarded the plane. We were still waiting for the coaching staff, so there was no threat of takeoff as I headed back to the person who'd called me.

Victor Garcia, one of the pitchers, was the one waving me over.

Unfortunately, he was sitting across the aisle from Silas. This 737 was owned by the team and had only two seats on each side of the aisle per row. When I stopped next to Garcia, Silas and Jenner were in the two seats across the aisle at my back. Or my side, rather, but whatever.

"What's up?" I asked him.

I'd put on my comfortable traveling outfit this morning, much like the one I'd worn on the trip to

Florida. Capri pants with the boyfriend roll and a Kalamazoo Knights T-shirt. Though today, I'd pulled my hair back into a ponytail because of the god-awful heat and humidity.

"You know my wife and I just had a baby."

"Sure do. Congratulations again." Not sure what this information had to do with me.

"She wants to go to the Boston series next month, but with the new baby and the three-year-old… traveling is—"

"A nightmare," I finished for him. "Your wives all get shafted on this stuff."

He nodded and didn't disagree. In season, baseball wives were almost single parents, given how much time was spent at the park or traveling for the players. Now, baseball careers didn't last a lifetime, so it was a short-term hardship on the WAGs (Wives and Girlfriends) for a long-term profit since the players were paid so well. Still, it was rough.

"I was wondering if there's anything you can do to help make her travel the easiest," he said.

I shook my head. "You know I can't book travel for the families."

"I know." He held his hand up. "I just meant pointers or maybe how to pick the best flight for traveling with the kids."

"I think the best thing would be to leave them with Grandma and Grandpa." That was what I would've done. My dad would take my kid for a weekend in a heartbeat. In some ways, I thought he couldn't wait to be a grandpa.

"Not an option. Her parents are out in Boston, so she'll have someone once she gets there and mine are in Arizona."

I sighed. "I can look into some things. Make some recommendations, but I can't book anything."

"Wouldn't expect you to."

"Send me her email address so I can get the information to her."

"Will do." He gave me a fake salute, making me laugh before I turned to walk away. "Silas said your tender heart wouldn't let you say *no*."

I turned quickly in just enough time to see Silas reach out and shove Garcia's shoulder. Then I steeled my gaze on him for the first time since that day.

Imaginary death lasers were shooting out of me. He had to have seen it because Jenner did and cackled like a little kid.

Tender heart, my ass.

The flight wasn't long and unlike the guys, I

could go home. Which I did before Silas or Jenner could catch up to me.

And my bed would feel like a little slice of heaven.

The team usually left wherever they were playing right after the game. Once the guys showered and changed, anyway. That way, everyone could spend an extra night in their own beds before the game the next day.

Baseball players only got rare days off during the season.

Once I'd showered the Florida day off me and was in my pajamas—a pair of shorts and T-shirt—I called my dad. Rather, I used Facetime so that I could see him.

He answered on the second ring.

"How was Florida?" he asked instead of saying *hello*. Dad had insisted on knowing my schedule for when I would be out of town with the team just so he wouldn't worry. As his only surviving child, I made it my mission to do everything I could so he wouldn't worry.

"Hot. Sticky."

He chuckled. "Sounds about right. What about everything else?" That was about Silas.

Dad knew I wasn't happy about having to see

him and had told me it'd be fine. That'd I'd survive it, which I had.

"Fine. I didn't have to see him much. Ignored him during the game. Didn't cheer for him."

"Ouch." But there was humor in his tone and on his face. "That had to smart."

"Dad! He—"

"I know, sweetheart. Not saying he didn't earn it. Just saying that it'd smart to have the woman you love refuse to cheer for you. He got a home run today, didn't he?"

I tightened my jaw and stared at him until he laughed again.

"First, he never said he loved me. You know that. Second, I don't know that he noticed."

"He noticed," he said immediately. "And I know he didn't tell you. Doesn't mean he didn't feel it. I've known that boy a lot of his life and can read him pretty good. He loves you, honey. Maybe it didn't work out, but the man loves you."

"Anyway… I don't really want to talk about him." Because at this point, I couldn't allow myself to believe that he loved me. Not when I'd loved him longer than I should ever admit and in the end, it hadn't mattered.

"So you're sticking the job out?"

"I told you that was a moment of weakness." One time, I'd tossed around the idea that maybe I would have to get a different job because seeing Silas was going to be too hard. One time. It had only lasted minutes. "This job is too good, Dad."

"So you're not going to let some guy run you off."

"Hell no." Even if that guy *was* Silas. "He's not going to stop me."

There was a knock on the door and it was far too late for someone to be here. I wasn't expecting a food delivery or anything else. Dad must've seen it in my face.

"Who is that? Don't hang up until you check your peephole," he told me.

I nodded then took him with me to the door.

Silas stood on the other side with his dark hair messy like he'd run his fingers through it a few times and he was now wearing jeans and a black T-shirt instead of the dress clothes from the plane.

I ran on quiet feet away from the door. "It's Silas," I whispered to my dad. "Why in the hell would he be here this time of night?"

"I have an idea." But he sounded annoyed.

I scoffed. "Don't be gross. We're not together."

Dad groaned and ran his hand down his face. "Are you going to hear him out?"

"I don't know."

"Maybe he wants to apologize."

I scrunched up my face at him so he'd know I thought he was out of his mind. Had Silas ever apologized for his behavior? Not that I knew of. Of course, I didn't know how he was with other women.

"I'm going to answer the door so I can tell him to leave, Dad. Nothing more."

He knocked again.

"Listen," Dad said, leaning closer to the phone. "All I'm saying is that you might want to give him a chance to apologize, even if it doesn't change anything. It'll at least lessen the hurt feelings." Then he leaned back. "Or open the door, kick him in the balls, and slam it in his face. Either way. I'm not invested."

Except that he *was* invested. Anything that had to do with me, Dad was invested.

"Bye, Dad." I ended the call.

After setting my phone on the arm of the couch, I ran my hands through my hair quickly in case it had become a wreck since I'd showered. Then I went to the door.

Once the locks were undone, I opened it and pretended that Silas didn't look as sexy as hell standing on the other side. The fishbowl effect of the peephole did nothing to make him less attractive.

Without greeting him, I raised my eyebrows.

"Can I talk to you?" he asked quietly.

I stepped back and opened the door wider so that he could come through. Then I folded my arms under my breasts and was reminded that I wasn't wearing a bra. He noticed too, judging by the way his gaze jumped up to mine and heated me to the core.

When he didn't say anything, I asked, "I thought you wanted to talk to me? I don't have anything to say, so you're going to have to start."

"Right." He sighed and ran his hand through his hair the way I'd imagined he would've when I'd noticed his hair had been messy through the peephole. "Do you want to sit?"

"I'm fine standing. I assume you won't be here long."

"Right," he said again. "I'm sorry, Amity," he began. "I'm sorry that I didn't call you or respond to your texts the week I was in California. My head was fucked up and that's not an excuse. I should've told you what was going through my mind."

"Yes. You should have."

"I didn't want to leave you hanging like that. Sure as hell didn't want you worry that I was with someone else."

"That thought never seriously crossed my mind until the argument. At first I thought it was something else, but then the way you were acting, I started to think… maybe…"

"I know. And that's my fault. I wouldn't do that to you," he said. That was at least something I could believe. "If I could go back…"

"Yeah. But we can't." I quickly wet my lips. "I appreciate the apology. Thank you."

"I wasn't angry with you, even if I acted like it when I got back. I was fucking pissed at myself for what happened with your brother and the longer we were together, the closer it was getting that you'd definitely find out and hate me. I couldn't stand the idea of you hating me for that, so I guess I unknowingly decided to make you hate me for something else."

"I don't hate you, Silas," I said softly. He took just one step closer, his eyes widening. "I've talked to my dad. He told me what happened. My brother swerved. It wasn't your fault."

"Yeah." He scratched the back of his head and I didn't think I'd ever seen Silas look so uncomfortable. "Jenner and I can't even remember what he swerved at."

"I know. It was also Jayce's decision to come get the two of you. He could've called you a ride share, but he wanted to take care of his friends." Tears burned the back of my eyes the way they did whenever I talked about what had happened to my brother. "You shouldn't beat yourself up about it. He wouldn't want that. My dad doesn't want that. I don't want that."

"I know." He swallowed hard. "You don't blame me? I was the one who brought him out."

Now I was the one to close the distance between us and set my hand on his forearm, giving it a little squeeze. "He chose to go and he'd do it again if he could. Hell, I would've done it. It could've easily been me in that car."

His eyes squeezed closed and his jaw tightened. "Please don't say that. It's not an image I can deal with."

Right. Hadn't thought about that.

To ease whatever was going through his head, I

slipped my arms around his waist and laid my head on his chest as I hugged him as tightly as I could. He wrapped his arms around me, only he was stronger.

Then he kissed the top of my head and pulled back, but not far enough for my arms to drop.

"You said that I never told you I love you."

"You didn't." My gaze locked with his. "Then again, you also said that I only see what I want to see, implying that you showed me your feelings and I didn't see it."

"I tried."

"I saw it, Silas. I knew you had feelings for me. I just didn't know that it meant love. My dad said it is… was," I corrected myself.

"Is." Both of his hands cupped the sides of my cheeks and tilted my head to look up at him. "I love you, Amity Kincaid."

My entire body felt like it'd gotten a hit of electricity. I was warm inside, my heart racing, my stomach flipping over itself at the potential of what might've been happening here. He could kiss me and I wouldn't stop him, even if it was the last one.

"I love you, Amity. Maybe I fucked this whole thing up, but I fucking love you more than I thought I could love another person. I don't care what people say about me, what people think, except you. I want to be the kind of man you could want."

I furrowed my brows. "You are. I've wanted you for…" I fluttered my eyes closed at the weight of what was happening right here. "Longer than I should have. I love you, Silas. I've always loved you."

He leaned down so that his lips were almost brushing against mine when he asked, "Can you forgive me for being an asshole?"

A small giggle bubbled up from my chest. "I think I have many times."

A great smile spread across his lips because he knew it was true. The guys in high school could be unintentional jerks, but I'd forgive them each time because I'd known then it hadn't been directed at me.

"And now?"

"You can't do that again," I told him.

"Never." The word wasn't much more than a breath against my face.

"Then, yeah, I can—" My words were cut off by his mouth on mine.

Silas kissed me like he hadn't kissed me in a year, let alone days. He kissed me like he might never get the chance to do it again and wanted to make sure that he conveyed all of his feelings. He kissed me like he would need to get me naked in minutes and by the way he was walking us back toward my bedroom, that seemed to be the case.

The light was off in my room, but the shade was still open, so the moonlight spilled across the darkness like a knife cutting a cake.

Once we were on the bed, he didn't hesitate until he was sure he'd shown me how much he loved me. Several times.

He touched my body like he revered it. Like I was something he hadn't thought he'd get to touch again and now… I was under him, willing and ready to reciprocate all of his feelings.

It wasn't until three orgasms later that he finally let himself go.

We were snuggled together in my bed, under the covers, tired and happy. His fingers trailed up my arm and then back down, leaving a wave of goosebumps. It was the good kind of tickling and I wouldn't tell him to stop.

"My dad thought you were here for a booty call."

He chuckled. "A booty call?"

"Isn't that what his generation would call it?"

"I think so." Our voices were low, as if we

worried someone would hear us, but we were the only two people in my apartment. "How did he know I was here?"

"I was on the phone with him when you knocked. He didn't want me to hang up until I looked through the peephole. Safety and all that."

"Was he pissed?" Despite all the pressure he'd experienced, Silas had never worried about disappointing his own father, but he did sometimes worry about disappointing mine.

"No. He told me to hear you out."

"So I have him to thank for being in your bed right now."

I scrunched up my face. "I really don't want to think about it that way."

His tired laugh shook my body.

"Are you leaving?" I asked him because I really wanted him to stay.

"Can't. Too late. I have a game tomorrow. Need my beauty sleep."

Now I was the one to grin and thankfully, he wasn't looking at me at all.

In the morning, we'd have to face the world and go back to work and everything. But tonight, we got to be in this happy, little cocoon, all warm and satisfied.

Because Silas loved me and I loved him, we'd work through anything else that came up.

There wasn't much more to ask for than that.

Thank you for reading KISSING THE PLAYER! I hope you enjoyed Silas & Amity's love story.

The following is a list of characters from Kissing the Player and their books.

Urban & Everly is Wanting the Player

I'm thrilled to offer a sneak peek of Urban & Everly's romance: Wanting the Player

I'm not here for a long time so I'm not looking for a relationship.

Then I meet Everly and she's someone I could see as a regular thing while I am here. That's all she wants but when I'm the one that starts falling, I have to convince her that she's more important than getting away from my family.

BONUS SCENE

Dear Reader,

I hope you enjoyed Kissing the Player. Silas & Amity were so much fun for me and had me swooning, not to mention wanting to knock Silas' head off. I'm excited for you to read more about them.

I have a bonus scene for you as a thank you for reading. Just click the link below, sign up for my newsletter, and you'll get an email with the bonus scene.

SIGN UP HERE:
https://geni.us/KissingBonus

MEET FOREVER 18

You heard talk of Forever 18 in the Reckless Saints series, but if you'd like to meet those rock stars yourself, check out the books in the series.
It's an interconnected stand alone series

Forever Grayson
(Grayson & Lilac)
[one night stand]
https://geni.us/grayson

Forever London
(London & Charlotte)
[grumpy/sunshine]
https://geni.us/Foreverlondon

Forever Lennox
(Lennox & Avalon)
[brother's best friend]
https://geni.us/lennox

Forever Thatcher
(Thatcher & Modestie)

[friends to lovers]
https://geni.us/Thatcher

Forever Jamison
(Jenner & Camden)
[sworn off relationships]
https://geni.us/ForeverJamison

MEET PUSHING DAISIES

Daisy is the musical genius everyone is talking about. If you'd like a series of spicy rock stars, check out the books in the Pushing Daisies series.
It's an interconnected stand alone series

Daisy
(Daisy & Lawson)
[small age gap]
https://geni.us/pushingdaisies1

Van
(Van & Lexi)
[fake friends to lovers]
https://geni.us/Ptkp

Bonham
(Bonham & Jurnie)
[fake boyfriend]
https://geni.us/xXSiGs

Daltrey
(Daltrey & Ella)

[workplace romance]
https://geni.us/DaltreyPD

Mack
(Mack & Bri)
[best friend's brother]
https://geni.us/Mack

MEET COURTING CHOAS

The band that started it all.
It's an interconnected stand alone series

Cross
(Cross & Indie)
[forbidden romance]
https://geni.us/pushingdaisies1

Ransom
(Ransom & Bellamy)
[friends to lovers]
https://geni.us/Ptkp

Booker
(Booker & Paige)
[workplace romance]
https://geni.us/xXSiGs

Dixon
(Dixon & Barrett)
[workplace romance]
https://geni.us/DaltreyPD

After living under my father's rule, I'm about to break free.

My father has kept me on a short leash my entire life.

The Orin comes for me.

Finding out what he is… scares the hell out of me.

Finding out I'm his supposed mate… I don't know that I'll recover.

START READING MOONSTRUCK TODAY

Being the daughter of my people's leaders, I should understand protocol and appropriate behavior. Problem is, I understand both, I just don't follow them.

But I have a different plan.

There's a boy… now a man, who is supposed to be powerful. I want him on our side.

What I didn't know is that together, he and I might be unstoppable.

Now I just have to find him.

START READING THE GREMLIN PRINCE TODAY

I'm a witch. Or so they tell me.

Finding out I'm a witch isn't even the weirdest part of my day. Having the guy who hated me in high school stand before me to tell me that I am, is.

Somehow, I'm supposed to learn spells and how to ground myself to the elements, fight the fact that I want him like I want air, and not freak out that my parents are part of a shadow coven trying to pull me over to the dark side.

Yeah. No problem.

START READING CURSED MAGIC TODAY

THE HARBOR POINT SERIES

A new adult contemporary romance series

Meet Gio and Sal.
Two damaged men who meet the woman who can
set them right.

Then there's Cash.
He's not damaged but he's ready to do the healing
when he meets Gemma.

START READING LOVE BY THE SLICE TODAY

GAMBLING ON LOVE

A new adult romance series

Desperate times call for desperate measures so Flannery Tate is selling her virginity.

START READING HIGHEST BIDDER TODAY

Want to stay up to date with all things Heather Young-Nichols? Join her newsletter! You'll get all of the cover reveals, teasers, sales first!

https://www.heatheryoungnichols.com/get-the-goodies

Let's be friends on social media:
TikTok Instagram Facebook
@heatheryoungnichols

Searching for Heather's reader group?
Join Heather Young-Nichols' Treasures on Facebook:
https://www.facebook.com/groups/heatherstreasures1

Heather Young-Nichols is a USA Today Bestselling author of contemporary and paranormal romances. She writes swoony heroes and snarky heroines with a heap of romance.

When she's not writing, she's binging a show with her kids, watching base-ball, or snuggling with her cuddly animals.

Find Heather on Social Media or by visiting her website.

heatheryoungnichols.com

facebook.com/heatheryoungnicholsauthor

instagram.com/heatheryoungnichols

amazon.com/Heather-Young-Nichols/e/B00KK-TM54A

bookbub.com/authors/heather-young-nichols

tiktok.com/@heatheryoungnichols